ALSO BY CAROL HIGGINS CLARK

Burned

The Christmas Thief
(with Mary Higgins Clark)

Popped

Jinxed

Fleeced

Twanged

Iced

Snagged

Decked

He Sees You When You're Sleeping
(with Mary Higgins Clark)

Deck the Halls
(with Mary Higgins Clark)

CAROL HIGGINS CLARK

FLEECED

A REGAN REILLY MYSTERY

POCKET BOOKS
New York   London   Toronto   Sydney

POCKET BOOKS, a division of Simon & Schuster, Inc.
1230 Avenue of the Americas, New York, NY 10020

This book is a work of fiction. Names, characters, places and incidents are products of the author's imagination or are used fictitiously. Any resemblance to actual events or locales or persons living or dead is entirely coincidental.

ISBN-13: 978-1-4165-2349-9
ISBN-10:   1-4165-2349-9

This Pocket Books paperback edition February 2006

10 9 8 7 6 5 4 3 2 1

POCKET and colophon are registered trademarks of Simon & Schuster, Inc.

Tip-in illustration by Carlos Beltran

Manufactured in the United States of America

For information regarding special discounts for bulk purchases, please contact Simon & Schuster Special Sales at 1-800-456-6798 or business@simonandschuster.com.

Acknowledgments

I am pleased to acknowledge the people who have been "gems" in offering their encouragement and support in the writing of this book.

Special thanks to Roz Lippel, my editor and friend, who has guided me with her insight and advice every step of the way.

I'd also like to thank my agent, Nick Ellison, and foreign rights director, Alička Pistek. I am continually grateful to my publicist, Lisl Cade.

Praise goes to art director John Fulbrook, associate director of copyediting Gypsy da Silva, and in dear memory of copyeditor Carol Catt, whom we miss so much.

Finally, thanks to my family and friends, especially my mother, Mary Higgins Clark, who knows how joyous it is to finally reach the point of writing the acknowledgments.

You're all flawless diamonds.

For my mother, Mary Higgins Clark,
and my stepfather, John Conheeney,
with love

FLEECED

Regan Reilly glanced out the window of the plane she'd been on for the last five hours, thrilled to finally spot the skyline of Manhattan. It's great to be back, she thought. This is where I belong. For a lot of reasons. Not the least of which was her new beau—the head of the Major Case Squad in New York City—one Jack Reilly, who thank God was no relation.

A private investigator in Los Angeles, thirty-one-year-old Regan was planning to attend the crime convention that her mother, mystery writer Nora Regan Reilly, had organized with a handful of her fellow authors. Regan's father, Luke, the owner of three funeral homes in New Jersey, would be there too. It was at Christmastime, when her father had been kidnapped, that Regan had met Jack Reilly. They'd been involved in a coast-to-coast romance for three months.

"I'd do anything that would result in your happiness, Regan," Luke had joked—more than once since he was safely home—"even be kidnapped."

Yes, Jack makes me happy, Regan mused as the wheels of the plane smoothly hit the pavement and the pilot taxied to the gate with no delays.

At the baggage claim Regan was inordinately pleased that for once her suitcases were among the first to be spit down the chute. She hoisted them onto the cart she'd rented and hurried out to grab a cab. There was only one person on the taxi line. This is all so easy today, Regan thought. Too easy. Something's got to go wrong. But even though it was after five o'clock on a Thursday, her cab made great time getting into the city.

As they passed the Plaza Hotel and headed across Central Park South, Regan smiled. Almost there, she thought. She'd be joining her parents at the convention's opening cocktail party and then for dinner. Jack had an awards ceremony he had to attend out on Long Island, but she'd see him tomorrow.

Life was a regular bowl of cherries.

At her parents' apartment, Regan felt the familiar sense of comfort that she always experienced when she walked through the door. She quickly showered, changed into a black dress, the nighttime uniform in the city, and hurried out. The cocktail party was still in full swing. Nora spotted Regan the minute she arrived, her maternal instinct on its usual red alert.

"Regan, you're here!" Nora exclaimed happily as she hurried over to greet her only child.

Several hours later, Regan, Nora, and Luke were finishing a festive dinner at the Gramercy Tavern. All the tables were filled, and the bar was bustling.

"That was delicious," Regan said as she looked around the busy restaurant. "This is the perfect place to kick off the weekend. I don't get down to this neighborhood enough."

Little did she know that, less than two blocks away, a crime was taking place. A crime that would bring her back to Gramercy Park much sooner than she expected.

Nat Pemrod sat at the antique desk in the living room of his splendid penthouse apartment and sighed happily. A few feet away, the door to his safe was open, and all its contents were spread out lovingly in front of him. With a hint of mist in his eyes, he gazed down at his deceased wife, Wendy's, engagement and wedding rings; the pearls he had given her on their first anniversary; the silly little ring they'd gotten out of a Cracker Jack box that Wendy had always treasured even more than her real jewelry. All the bracelets and earrings and necklaces and pins he had bought her over the years were here. Each and every bauble and trinket, cheap or expensive, held a special memory.

Nat had been a jeweler for fifty years. A few days ago, he and his buddy and fellow jeweler Ben had decided to donate the proceeds from the sale of four precious diamonds they'd owned secretly for almost half a century to their ailing Settlers' Club in honor of its one hundredth anniversary.

They'd both been "Settlers" since their early thirties, and Nat had been in residence at the club for most of his life. The club, founded by an eccentric for "pioneering people with spirit," and located on beautiful Gramercy Park in New York City, had in its heyday been a favored gathering place for social, political, and artistic leaders, a mecca for cultural events. Its membership of "pioneers" had consisted of men and women with a broad range of occupations and personalities, and included a fair share of oddballs. But now the club was suffering the fate of many similar clubs and was in danger of closing. Membership was down, the place was in disrepair, and funds were low. It was sneeringly referred to by some as the "Settled Down Club."

With the anniversary party coming up, Nat and Ben had decided they should put their money where their hearts were, so to speak, sell their diamonds, and fork over what would amount to four million dollars to the club.

"It should certainly help get this joint jumping again." Nat chuckled.

Nat had also decided it was high time to make some final decisions about who would get Wendy's jewelry. When he was gone, he wanted the baubles to be appreciated. But while he was alive he couldn't bear the thought of Wendy's jewels adorning another woman's body. He conducted his private, loving inventory and was about to put the jewelry back in the safe when once again his eyes fell on the special red-velvet jewelry case.

Nat's hands trembled slightly as he reached for it. Cradling the case in his outstretched palms, he opened it carefully and stared at the four large and brilliant diamonds that in a matter of days would be turned into cold, hard cash. "I hate to say good-bye to you guys after fifty years of togetherness, but this club of ours really needs the dough." Nat laughed and placed the box back down on the desk.

A surge of excitement coursed through his veins, and he clapped his hands. This is going to be fun, he thought. Helping this club fix itself up. The big one hundredth anniversary party on Saturday night. More parties to celebrate throughout the year. Ben and I will be at the helm of it all. It sure brightens up a dreary March.

The raw wind outside suddenly seemed to penetrate the apartment. Nat pulled his bathrobe closer and looked around at his living room appreciatively. The glorious wood paneling, the antique furniture, the wrought iron staircase that led up to a balcony with floor-to-ceiling bookshelves, the tops of which overlooked the couch, the fireplace, and the pair of life-sized sheep that were perched in front of the window.

Nat and Wendy had bought them early in their marriage because they reminded her of her childhood days on a sheep farm in England. Over the years, Nat had surprised her with any sheep knickknacks he could get his hands on. But the two stuffed sheep were her favorites. They were the children she never had. She loved them so much that when she made a generous donation to the Settlers' Club right before she died three years ago, it was with the understanding that when she and Nat were both dead, the club would take those sheep and put them in a place of honor in the front parlor.

Yes indeed, this has been a wonderful place to

live for more than fifty years, Nat thought. Ben and I made the right decision to be such generous souls and make sure it keeps going!

He jumped up, grabbed the red box, and walked over to the sheep, whom he and Wendy had named Dolly and Bah-Bah. He pulled the two glass stones out of Dolly's eye sockets and replaced them with two of the diamonds. He then repeated the procedure on Bah-Bah, stood back, and smiled.

"The eyes have it!" He laughed. "You two look like a million bucks. Your mama, Wendy, loved it when you slept with the diamonds in your eyes. She said you were her precious jewels. This is one of the last nights your eyes will have that special sparkle."

Carefully, Nat pulled the strands of wool that were their bangs over their now valuable eyes and patted them both. He dropped the glass stones into the red box and replaced it on the desk.

I'll take my shower and then close up shop here, he thought with a smile. He shuffled down the long hallway and through his bedroom. In the opulent marble master bathroom, Nat turned on the jets in the shower full force.

"That'll feel good on these old bones," he muttered as he walked past the oversize Jacuzzi and back into his bedroom, closing the bathroom door behind him. "Warm it up a little in there first," he said.

The ten o'clock news would just be starting. He lay down on his bed, grabbed the remote control, and flicked on the television. What a day, he thought, chuckling happily. Making plans to give away several million bucks can really tire you out. Nat closed his eyes for what he thought would be a moment but quickly dozed off. When he awoke with a start, the clock on the bedside table read 10:38.

Nat pulled his eighty-three-year-old body up and slid down off the old-fashioned four-poster bed that his dear wife had purchased three decades ago at a most serendipitous garage sale. As he pushed open the bathroom door, a wall of steam enveloped him. "Ahhhhhh," he grunted as he took off his bathrobe and hung it on a hook.

But something was wrong. He peered through the steam and stepped toward the Jacuzzi. It was filled with water. "What?" he said aloud as fear clutched his heart. "I didn't turn this on . . . did I?"

"No, you didn't."

Startled, Nat spun around. He started to speak, but before the words came out, an intruder emerged from the steam and gave Nat a forceful shove that sent him hurtling backward into the Jacuzzi. Nat's head banged against the side of the tub before it slid below the surface of the water.

"Perfect." The intruder watched as Nat's body settled into a nearly motionless state, swaying ever so gently with the movement of the slowly calming water. "It's a shame how many people lose their lives when they slip in the tub. A crying shame."

A moment later, the shower jets were turned off and the inside of the stall had been wiped dry.

2

If just this morning someone had said to Thomas Pilsner, "Have a nice day," he would have responded in the usual robotic fashion that most of the rest of the world did when they heard the clichéd phrase.

What a difference twelve hours makes.

How could he have known that at lunchtime two members of the club where he was president would give him the greatest news in the world? The Settlers' Club, which needed repairs like nobody's business and had been in serious danger of running out of operating money, was going to get what would probably amount to four million dollars.

How's that for a shot in the arm? Thomas thought to himself. It was eleven o'clock at night and he had felt electrified since lunch. He was working late, going over everything that had to be done before the big party on Saturday night. What a celebration it would be! Nat and Ben had told him they wanted to do a special presentation of the diamonds at the party.

"Anything you want!" Thomas had said with a fierceness he almost didn't recognize in himself. He'd practically done a jig around town this afternoon when he was running his errands. He hadn't told anyone yet, but he suspected the news had leaked. But who cared? All's well that ends well. The party would be exciting no matter what.

The phone on his desk rang. That must be my little Janey, he thought. Janey was his girlfriend of six months, and they usually talked several times a day. They'd met when she attended a lecture at the club, and everyone agreed they were perfect for each other. She was never without a strand of pearls and a cardigan sweater. He was never without his trademark bow tie. Both only in their twenties, they felt like old souls who had been together in another lifetime, who really belonged in a bygone era. Sometimes they discussed how they would have loved to live in New York City in the 1890s. But the time they had treated themselves to a horse-and-buggy ride in Central Park, in an attempt to re-create the past, they'd been surrounded by sweaty joggers and an obnoxious Rollerblader who kept circling the buggy.

It didn't take long after Thomas answered the phone for his face to fall. "Ben Carney? Oh no . . ."

Thomas ran out of his office, down the hallway, and frantically pressed the elevator button. The door slowly rumbled open, slowly rumbled shut, and the ancient elevator creaked its way upstairs to the fourth floor. Another thing that needs to be replaced, Thomas thought in the midst of his anguish. How could he break the news to Nat about his old friend Ben?

When the door opened again, Thomas ran down the hallway to Nat Pemrod's apartment and rang the bell. The sounds of another one of Lydia Sevatura's singles parties echoed from across the hall. The gauche things I have to put up with so that this club might attract new members, he thought.

Nat didn't answer.

Thomas rang again.

When Nat still didn't answer, he put his ear to the door. He thought he could hear the faint sound of the television. Thomas reached in his pocket and pulled out the master key he always carried in case of emergencies. He unlocked the door and entered cautiously. To the left of the foyer was the hallway leading to the bedrooms and the kitchen and dining room. To the right was the archway to the living room that extended the length of the apartment.

"Nat?" he called. As he approached Nat's bedroom, the sound of the television got louder. "Nat?"

At the doorway of the bedroom, Thomas peered in. Pillows were propped up against the headboard, and the bedspread was rumpled. Thomas's throat went dry. He walked into the bathroom. A scream, barely audible, escaped his mouth.

His feet carried him quickly back down the hall and out the front door, just as the door to Lydia's apartment opened. He felt breathless as he ran to the end of the hallway, through the fire door, and took the steps three at a time, down to the first floor. In his office he dialed 911 as fast as his fingers could move.

Within minutes the police and Nat's private doctor arrived on the scene. Back upstairs, Thomas watched in horror as the doctor pronounced Nat dead.

"He slipped in the tub," Dr. Barnes said. "It looks like blunt trauma to the head. He's been having some dizzy spells lately . . ."

Just then, one of the patrolmen walked into

the bedroom. "There's a lot of jewelry out on the desk in the living room. The safe is empty."

Thomas looked up. "He told me he and his friend Ben were about to sell the four big diamonds in the red box and donate the proceeds to the club."

"I didn't see any red box."

"But they just showed it to me this afternoon!"

"Believe me, there's no red box. A lot of dark blue boxes. But no red box."

Thomas promptly fainted.

3

Regan Reilly opened the door of her parents' apartment and picked up the three daily newspapers that had been plopped on the floor at some ungodly hour while most of New York City was unconscious. Backing into the apartment, Regan shut the door and made her way into the narrow kitchen. She opened the cabinet over the sink and pulled out a mug as the coffeemaker hissed and groaned, spitting the last couple of freshly brewed drops into the glass pot. Music to my ears, Regan thought. It means that caffeine is just seconds from my bloodstream.

Regan settled herself at the dining room table and took that first, best sip of coffee. Her eyes took in the unbelievable view of Central Park that her mother always said made the apartment. It certainly does, Regan thought. Her parents' pied-à-terre was a comfortable two-bedroom place to hang your hat, but it was the floor-to-ceiling windows overlooking the park from the sixteenth floor that made it to die for. And even on this cold and gray March morning, the view of the park was mesmerizing.

Coffee, the papers, and Central Park. A great way to start the day. And before the day is over, I'll get to see Jack, she thought. She was suddenly reminded of a discussion held in one of her college English classes. Expectation and anticipation are one half the joy of life. Regan smiled. True most of the time. But being with Jack was a whole lot better than looking forward to it. I've had enough of looking forward! she thought. It's time to live.

Regan opened one of the tabloids, a paper she always enjoyed reading when she was in New York City. The first few pages included the usual stories about conflicts of varying degrees of seriousness taking place in the Big Apple. Crackdowns on motorists who cause gridlock and jaywalkers who dart in and out of the gridlock, a bank robbery in midtown, noise from a construction site that had the neighbors going crazy.

Then Regan turned the page and gasped. In the middle of the page was a picture of her with her mother at last night's opening cocktail party for the crime convention. A brief writeup described the plans for the four-day affair.

The caption under the picture read: "Mystery writers gather today through Sunday to hear experts in all aspects of crime fighting share their expertise. Bestselling mystery writer Nora Regan Reilly is chairman of the convention. Daughter Regan is no stranger to law enforcement. She is a private investigator who jetted into town from her Los Angeles home to attend the lectures and seminars, and, of course, the festivities."

Los Angeles home! Regan thought. A one-bedroom apartment. Jetted into town! Coach class on a flight that served ice-cold bagels. Whoever said it's all an illusion wasn't kidding. At least the picture was pretty good.

Regan, classified as Black Irish thanks to her dark hair, light skin, and blue eyes, had her arm around her mother who, at five feet three inches tall, was three inches shorter than Regan. They looked like mother and daughter, although Nora was a blonde. Regan had inherited her coloring from her father, whose hair was now a distinguished silver but had been dark in his youth. Luke was six feet five inches, so Regan's height favored neither parent's lineage. Since she was an only child, Regan was the sole result of the blending of their genes. Talk about the quintessential crapshoot.

"That coffee smells great."

Regan turned to see her mother standing in the doorway of the kitchen, a pale pink silk robe wrapped around her slender frame. Her face, devoid of makeup, had a serene beauty. She yawned and reached for a china cup and saucer in the cabinet next to her. There was something about staying in the New York apartment that made Nora always want to use the good dishes. Regan thought it might be the view of the park that did it. When you drank from a china cup early in the morning, you felt as if you could be in a glamorous movie from the forties. Not a plastic cup or beer can in sight.

"Anything interesting in the paper?"

"If you think we're interesting, then the answer would have to be yes."

"Huh?" Nora peered over Regan's shoulder.

Regan pointed to the picture. "Mommy and me."

Nora laughed. "How sweet," she said as she squinted and leaned down to examine it. "That's good publicity for the convention. I want to get down to the Paisley this morning before ten. I'm sure there'll be late registrants straggling in."

The Paisley was an old, midsize hotel off of Seventh Avenue in the mid-fifties that had clearly seen better days. But it had a certain musty charm and was the perfect size for the convention. It was big enough to handle all the seminars, but small enough to be cozy. Nora had made a deal with the hotel that included free coffee and as many folding chairs as there were behinds to fill them.

The phone rang. Regan glanced over at the clock on the mantel. "It's not even eight o'clock yet. I wonder who that could be?"

"I hope it's not bad news," Nora said anxiously as she straightened up and reached for the phone on the kitchen wall.

We're so Irish, Regan thought. What was that line? The Irish have an abiding sense of tragedy that gets us through the good times. Which meant that any phone call before 8:00 A.M. and after 11:00 P.M. could only mean big trouble. It was never even considered that it might be someone who wanted to talk when the rates were cheaper.

Regan watched the expression on her mother's face. As soon as Nora recognized the caller, she relaxed and smiled.

"Thomas, how are you?"

Thomas who? Regan wondered.

"That's all right. You're not disturbing us at all . . ."

Oh sure, Regan thought. Our hearts only skipped a few dozen beats. And that extra surge of adrenaline when the phone rang gave me a needed boost.

"Yes, Regan is right here. Let me put her on . . ." Nora handed Regan the phone. "It's Thomas Pilsner."

Regan's eyebrows raised. "Oh," she muttered with surprise. Thomas, a lovable eccentric, was the latest president of the Settlers' Club down in Gramercy Park. He and Regan had become fast friends when she attended a Mystery Writers dinner with her mother there last fall.

"Hi, Thomas," Regan said cheerfully, picturing his baby face and mop of light-brown hair that looked like one big wave. It seemed to Regan that he could step into a snapshot from a hundred years ago and not look out of place.

"Regan! Oh my God, Regan!" Thomas cried hysterically, apparently having kept his real feelings from her mother.

"Thomas, what's wrong?"

"I've barely slept all night. Then I saw your picture in the paper when it was delivered at six o'clock this morning, and I waited as long as I could to call you. Oh God!"

"Thomas, calm down. Tell me what's wrong."

"Last night two of our elderly members died."

"I'm sorry," Regan said, thinking that the Irish intuition about phone calls before 8:00 A.M. had for once proved to be true. She could just hear her grandmother crying triumphantly, "I told you!" "What happened to them?" she asked.

"One of them had a heart attack in front of a bus and the other slipped in the tub last night. But if you ask me, something smells about the whole thing." Thomas's voice was trembling, but his words came tumbling out in a torrent. "Not just smells. Reeks! I just had lunch with the two of them yesterday. They told me they planned to sell four valuable diamonds and donate the proceeds to the club. It would have meant about four million dollars for us."

"Well, won't that still happen?"

"The diamonds are missing!"

"Missing?"

Thomas relayed to Regan the story of everything that had happened the day before. "And the red box with the diamonds is not with the rest of the jewelry. It's gone."

"What do the police say?" Regan asked.

"Well, I'm not completely sure."

"Why not?"

"Because I fainted."

"Oh dear."

"It was so embarrassing. When I came to, they brought me downstairs to my apartment, and the doctor gave me a sedative and told me to get a good night's sleep. I was in shock."

"But you didn't get a good night's sleep."

"Lord, no! After a couple of hours I was wide awake again. It's bad enough to think that Nat and Ben are both gone, but I'm convinced that someone is trying to get away with murder and theft. The police think Nat just hit his head, but I think someone came in here and killed him and stole the diamonds."

"You don't have anything in writing about their intention to give the club the money from the diamonds?"

"No. This all came up just yesterday. It was going to be made public on Saturday night at our one hundredth anniversary party."

"But you saw the diamonds?"

"They were sitting next to my Cobb salad during most of lunch. Every once in a while they let me open up the box and stare at them. They were so beautiful."

"Could Ben have taken the diamonds home with him?" Regan asked.

"That would be bad too."

"Why?"

"Because his wallet was missing by the time they got him to the hospital. If he had the diamonds on him, they would surely have been taken along with his wallet. Luckily his Settlers' Club card was found in his pocket."

"That red box could be hidden in the apartment somewhere."

"I don't think so."

"Why not?"

"Because Nat mentioned at lunch that he was glad he wouldn't have to worry about forgetting the combination to the safe anymore."

"Why did they own the diamonds together?"

"They were both jewelers. They were part of a group of four jewelers who played cards together every week for fifty years in Nat's apartment. They called themselves the Suits, after the spades, hearts, clubs, and diamonds in the deck. Of course the diamonds were their favorite. Way back when, they'd each brought the most beautiful, valuable diamond they owned to one of the games. They made a pact not to tell anyone about these jewels—except for Wendy, Nat's wife, who was in the apartment that night—and the last one alive would get to keep all four diamonds. Survivor takes all, they called it. Well, two of them died last year before I started this job. They belonged to the club too. With the centennial anniversary coming up, Nat and Ben decided to do some good with the diamonds and not wait until just one of them was left alive to enjoy the money. But now they're both dead!"

"I wonder what the police are thinking?" Regan said.

"They probably think that I took them!"

"Why would you say that?"

"Because I knew about them."

"But you brought it up to them. Didn't you say the diamonds' existence had been pretty much a secret?"

"Word had definitely leaked in the club. There were cries and whispers, Regan. Cries and whispers! People heard about the plans for Saturday. Maybe it was the waiter, I don't know. If I hadn't brought it up, and they're not donated to the club, people would ask where they are! It would look like I was hiding them for myself."

"I see," Regan said.

"Could that make me a suspect?"

Regan cleared her throat. "Thomas, the police always take a look at everyone who might have had the motive or the opportunity to carry out a crime."

"That's why I need you, Regan."

"What do you want me to do?"

"Regan, please come stay here. Help me solve

this mess. Help me get back those diamonds. Help me clear my name. Help me secure the future of the Settlers' Club!"

Is that all? Regan wondered. "Thomas, I'm only in town for a few days. I have to get back to Los Angeles on Monday. I'm in the middle of a case."

"I don't care! Come for the weekend then. See what you can figure out in the little time you have." He paused and said plaintively, "I need you, Regan. I don't know what else to do."

Regan looked over at her mother, who was sitting at the table, studying Regan with a quizzical look.

"Okay, Thomas," Regan said. "I'll come stay with you. I can be down there by about ten."

"Regan, I knew you were the one to call. You'll get to the bottom of this."

"I hope I don't disappoint you, Thomas. I'll do my best." When Regan hung up the phone, she turned to her mother. "You always said you wanted me to work in New York City."

4

Here we are, Princess of Love," Maldwin Feckles declared as he carried a tray with hot coffee, freshly squeezed orange juice, and flakey croissants into his employer's darkened bedroom. "Time to rise and shine and fix people up." He placed the tray on a table next to the king-size bed and opened the drapes.

Lydia's eyes fluttered as she groaned. "What time is it?"

"It's 8:00 A.M. The time you instructed me to serve you breakfast."

"Was I dreaming, or did what happened last night really happen?"

Maldwin sighed. He was a short man with rigid posture, tufts of dark hair that given half a chance would be sprouting willy-nilly from the sides of his head but were held in place by industrial-strength gel, and a face of baby-smooth white skin. "I'm afraid our neighbor Nat did in fact pass over."

"'Pass over' isn't the word," Lydia said as she sat up. "He departed this planet in a most dramatic fashion." Her mouth broke into a wide yawn as she reached for the pink feather bed jacket that went over the top of her pink silk nightgown. Ever since she inherited two million dollars from an elderly neighbor in Hoboken she'd not only moved into a penthouse apartment in New York City, but she'd also launched a full scale dating service, aptly named Meaningful Connections, with matchmaking parties held in her own elegant home. She'd also decided that she must always dress the part of the Princess of Love.

It was all so hard to believe.

At the ripe old age of thirty-eight, Lydia's wildest dreams had come true. She'd gone from living in a little studio apartment on the wrong side of the tracks to having a butler who was devoted to her. All because she'd run some errands for Mrs. Cerencioni, who seemed as if she didn't have enough money to pay the light bill.

Of course, Lydia had unfortunately hooked up with a golddigger who was her boyfriend for about five minutes before she managed to shake him loose. But he still left messages on her machine and sent love notes in the mail. It was wildly embarrassing.

But now things could get even worse. After all the money she'd invested into fixing up the apartment and setting up her business, there was the danger that the club might have to close its doors and sell the building. Just when she and Maldwin were getting their respective businesses on track, she'd have to find a new place to live and work. And to think the club could have been saved by the diamonds they'd heard all the gossip about last night and that now were among the missing.

"All that confusion and death," Lydia said as she picked up her orange-juice glass and tapped it with her long red fingernails. "Do you think people might be afraid to come to my parties now?"

Maldwin fluffed the pillow behind her dyed blond hair. "It was excitement that can only help. No one will ever accuse you of throwing parties that are dull. After all, matchmaking should have an air of mystery."

"But what if the papers report that some of my guests were disturbed by the arrival of the police?"

"As long as they spell your name right. And the name of my butler school," Maldwin sniffed. "Miss Lydia, remember what we decided when we joined forces."

"There's no such thing as bad publicity."

"Exactly." Maldwin walked to the door of the bedroom.

"But Maldwin, I'm worried."

Maldwin waited.

"If we have to find a new place to live, it'll be very expensive. My stationery cost a fortune. And people get used to coming to a certain location for these parties. Being in Gramercy Park gave them a certain je ne sais quoi."

Maldwin flinched. He couldn't stand it when she threw in her schoolgirl French. Her accent was awful.

"I know, Princess," he said. "But we must go on. Tomorrow night's party should attract new members to the club. And hopefully, those diamonds will be recovered and we can continue on as we are now." He smoothed back his hair and adjusted his pinkie ring. "My students are arriving soon. We're leaving for a field trip to a town full of antique shops in western New Jersey. I expect we'll be back later this afternoon."

Lydia grumbled. "And I'm going to exercise class. Don't forget. Tonight we have to go to Stanley's studio for the interview. He wants to air the special on the club and us this Sunday night. How many viewers does he have on that cable show?"

"I'm afraid neighborhood free-access channels do not draw the masses, Princess of Love. But it's a start."

"I've come a long way from my studio apartment with no closet space," Lydia mused. "And Maldwin, I don't want to go back."

"We will make our businesses flourish, Miss Lydia," Maldwin said formally, "at any cost."

They laughed nervously together. He gave a short, courtly bow and shut the door.

5

Regan stepped out of the shower, dressed quickly, and dried her hair. She turned off the hair dryer, placed it on her dresser, and heard her cell phone ringing.

It was Jack. Regan smiled at the sound of his voice. She pictured his face with its hazel eyes and even features, framed by sandy hair that curled at the ends. He was six feet two inches tall, with broad shoulders and an undeniable charisma. Keenly intelligent and quick-witted, he also had a sense of humor that had developed from growing up in a large family. Thirty-four years old, Jack had been raised in Bedford, New York, graduated from Boston College, and had surprised his family by following his grandfather into the field of law enforcement.

Jack's grandfather had been a New York police lieutenant. In the twelve years since college, Jack had risen through the ranks from patrolman to captain and head of the Major Case Squad. He had also picked up two master's degrees, and his goal was to become police commissioner of New York.

"How was your dinner last night?" Regan asked.

"Let's just say I would rather have been with you. I heard a lot of boring speeches, then drove back to the city from Long Island. I didn't get home until almost two."

"Well, you'll never believe what I've gotten involved in."

"I was about to say the same thing."

Regan sat on the bed. "You first."

Jack paused. "I have to fly to London tonight. There's a case over there I have to take a look at for my buddy at Scotland Yard. But I'll be back by Sunday."

Regan felt a sharp stab of disappointment. I guess I'll get to enjoy more expectation and anticipation, she thought, but said, "I'm leaving Monday."

"I know. I'm coming with you."

Regan laughed. "Oh really?"

"If you'll have me. I get a few days off and I want to be with you."

"I want to be with you too," Regan said. "L.A. on Monday sounds great."

"What did you get yourself involved in?" Jack asked. "There's not another man, I hope."

Regan laughed. "Another guy called but it's not anything to worry about." She relayed to him the conversation with Thomas.

"So you're on the job this weekend too. Let me pick you up and take you down to Gramercy Park," Jack said quickly. "I can't wait until Sunday to see you."

"I was about to say the same thing."

Jack laughed. "I'll be there in half an hour."

Regan hung up the phone. There is a God, she thought.

6

Thomas Pilsner sat at his desk in his office on the first floor of the Settlers' Club, wringing his hands. Normally the sight of his Oriental rug, faded leather club chairs, and handsome rolltop desk soothed him. But not today. His mind was racing, and his heart was beating at a rate that would only have been acceptable if he had just finished a run around Gramercy Park.

How he loved it here. Gramercy Park, with its graceful trees, shady lawns, cast-iron gates, and flagstone sidewalks, was like a mirage just steps from Midtown Manhattan. The park was the cloistered centerpiece of the neighborhood. It was a landmark that had been called the cherished jewel in the crown that is New York City. Original town houses in Greek Revival, Italianate, Gothic

Revival, and Victorian Gothic surrounded the park, and one of the city's earliest apartment houses had been built on its southeast corner.

Everyone who lived on the square received a key to the gate of the private park—a two acre haven of pastoral charm, accessible only to bordering property owners.

People felt as if they were stepping into another century when they rounded the corner and the park came into view. Noise receded, and time moved much more slowly. The chaos and confusion of the city seemed to disappear as the skyscrapers and traffic jams were left behind.

This place feels like anything but a haven now, Thomas thought miserably. *Why didn't I live here a hundred years ago, when the writers and painters and architects all made their homes in these beautiful buildings and life was so much more civilized? When the club didn't have all these financial difficulties?*

Thomas blew his nose and willed himself to be calm. *Regan's coming,* he thought. *She'll help me with all this.*

The phone on his desk rang.

"Regan Reilly is here," the security guard told him.

"Send her in."

* * *

Jack's arm was around Regan's shoulder as he guided her up the staircase to the main floor and down the hall to Thomas's office.

"This doesn't sound like it qualifies for the Major Case Squad, but I'm anxious to hear what's going on," he said to Regan.

Thomas greeted them at the door. "Regan," he cried, "not a moment too soon."

Regan introduced Thomas to Jack. They sat down in the chairs across the desk from Thomas.

"Jack has to leave soon," Regan said, "but he's with the Major Case Squad in Manhattan and is a good friend of mine. He's here to help us."

Thomas gave Jack the once-over. "I need all the help I can get."

"I've already filled Jack in on everything you told me," Regan said. "What else can you tell us about what's been going on around here?"

"I was hired last September, after I graduated from business school, to try and bring some new life to this club. The place might not look it on the surface, but it's falling apart! It needs so much work, and it needs new members. With all the health clubs springing up, people aren't joining the old clubs anymore."

Regan nodded her head as if urging him to continue.

"I've done everything I can to drag people in

here. A movie company is even using the front
parlor this afternoon to shoot scenes for their latest film. We're having a gala anniversary party
here tomorrow night. The club is one hundred
years old. That's why Nat and Ben decided to
make the donation now. It would have brought
such excitement and publicity. It was our only
chance. I'd even lined up a couple of reporters to
come over and cover the party. But now there's no
donation, and I have to try and hide the fact that
there was probably a murder and a robbery here!
Who would want to join a club where these terrible things have happened?" Thomas broke the
pencil he was holding in his hands and dropped
the pieces on the desk. His upper lip was starting
to sweat.

"How many apartments are on this guy's
floor?" Regan asked.

"Just two. They're the penthouses."

"Was there anyone home across the hall last
night?" Jack asked.

Thomas rolled his eyes. "Was there ever! The
woman who lives there has singles parties. She
started a matchmaking service. She was having a
little do last night."

"Well, someone from the party could have gotten access to Pemrod's apartment," Regan suggested.

"She also has a butler who runs a butler school up there. He only has a few students, but they were working at the party. When the police helped me downstairs after I fainted, everyone was standing around. It was terrible!"

"Could you have left the door open when you ran downstairs after discovering Nat's body?" Regan asked. "There would have been time for someone to steal the diamonds and get out before the police arrived."

"I suppose," Thomas said slowly. "I was in such a state. It's not every day that you find someone floating in the tub. I should just have called the police from there . . ."

Regan sighed. "Were there people in the hall-way before word got out about Nat's death?"

"People were going out to the terrace at the end of the hall to smoke. Lydia doesn't let people smoke in her apartment."

"And people had heard about the existence of the diamonds?" Jack asked.

"Apparently the place was buzzing with the news."

"Maybe Nat or Ben told someone of their plans," Regan said. "That's the kind of secret that's hard to keep. What about Nat's next of kin?"

"I just spoke to his only relative, a brother who

lives in Palm Springs. His name is Carl Pemrod. He knew nothing about the diamonds. He can't travel anymore, so he won't make it out here. Nat's body will be cremated. Carl wants you to call him, Regan. I have his number for you. He met your mother once when she spoke at the library out there. He said you're welcome to stay in the apartment and do what you need to do."

Regan raised her eyes. "Stay in the apartment?"

"Yes. There was a flood in our guest suite in the basement, and it smells kind of musty. Or else you can stay in my apartment, but I only have one bedroom. I can sleep on the couch."

"No," Regan said almost too quickly. "I'll stay up there. I assume the police have no problem with that."

"They didn't declare it a crime scene! I wish they had!"

"It has two bedrooms and baths?" Regan asked.

"Yes."

"Good. I'd prefer not to use the bathroom he was found in."

The phone on Thomas's desk rang. As he picked it up, Jack reached over and grabbed Regan's hand. "I've got to go. Walk outside with me."

Regan followed him out into the hallway, down the steps, and out the front door. The day suddenly felt chillier, and the sky was a more ominous gray.

Jack reached over and pulled on the lapels of Regan's jacket. "I wish I didn't have to go away."

"Not more than me." Regan leaned her head against Jack's shoulder. "That apartment is going to be lonely and eerie when I'm here all by myself."

Jack laughed and put his arms around her. "Lock the doors, baby. I'm going to call over to the 13th Precinct and talk to whoever was here last night. As soon as I do, I'll let you know and get you the reports. Stay in touch with those guys."

"Well, it sounds to me like this is going to be my investigation. It doesn't seem like they're pursuing it."

"No sign of forced entry. Jewelry left out. No letter of intent about the diamonds. Old guy slips in the tub. They might be operating under the assumption that there was no crime."

"But I believe Thomas. Those diamonds have to be somewhere."

"Even if they are, if the bequest isn't in Nat's will, then the diamonds would go to his brother."

Regan shrugged. "I'll look into it all." She

smiled up at him. "I think we're both going to have some weekend."

Jack leaned down and kissed her. "Sunday will be the best part."

Regan turned and peered up at the club. It had a slightly foreboding look. "If I make it to Sunday," she said.

7

It was a wet, cold day in the rolling hills of Devon, England. Rain pelted mournfully against the windows of Thorn Darlington's country estate, home of his famous butler school. Thorn had been in a bad mood for several weeks, coinciding with the commencement of Maldwin Feckles's butler classes over in New York City.

"I know his school will be pathetic, but he's doing this to ruin me!" Thorn had cried when he heard the news. "He knew that I was planning to open a branch of the Thorn Darlington School for Butlers there next year. He's stealing my thunder! On purpose!"

Thorn sank his rotund body into a leather club chair that squeaked in protest whenever he sat down. He sipped the tea that his own butler had just delivered. His whole body ached. The dreary weather seemed to have seeped into his bones, and the aggravations of the day were driving him over the edge. His Thorn Darlington School for Butlers, which had been in existence for over thirty-five years, was about to begin the two-week refresher course that was worse than the six-week intensive program. The course was often filled with a bunch of "know-it-alreadys." Thorn knew that all they wanted was the Thorn Darlington certificate, which would naturally increase their chances of finding a proper butlering job. Thorn put up with their attitudes because, after the course, most of them would find jobs through Thorn's placement agency.

He had quite a racket going.

Thorn bit into a tasty shortbread cookie. As he chewed, the frown on his face grew deeper and deeper, while his bushy eyebrows twitched up and down. Just thinking about Maldwin Feckles's nerve drove him nuts. And now he'd heard that Maldwin was getting publicity for that bloody school, publicity that should have been reserved for him. Feckles was going to be on television in New York City with his students. It was maddening!

Many new butler schools had tried to imitate the Thorn Darlington School, attempting to steal business from him, but they had all quickly shut their doors, failing miserably after one mishap or another. Now Thorn was ready to conquer New York, and he had no intention of letting an odd-ball wanna-be like Maldwin Feckles get in his way.

In the fall, Maldwin had taken Thorn's refresher course but had stormed out of Thorn's office when he realized he was not among the applicants being sent to interview for a job he desperately wanted. He had said he was going to make Thorn very sorry.

Thorn had just snorted and laughed.

Maldwin took off for a holiday in New York City, where he accidentally landed a butlering job, then started his classes. And so far, Thorn had not been able to do anything to stop him.

The phone on the table next to him jangled, fraying his nerves to the breaking point. With great irritation, he answered it.

A few moments later the first broad smile in weeks spread across his jowly face. "A suspicious death and possible burglary right across the hall from Maldwin's butler school? How delicious! I don't think it will be too hard to stir up a bit more trouble around there now, do you?" Thorn's infrequent laugh bellowed through his gloomy office. "Old Maldwin Feckles is going to be very, very sorry he ever stuck his nose into the business of running a butler school. Very sorry indeed."

8

Daphne Doody had lived in an apartment on the ground floor of the Settlers' Club for nearly twenty years, but in all that time she had never seen anything that could compare to the excitement of the last twenty-four hours.

First the news about the generous donation that was to be made by Nat Pemrod and Ben Carney had spread through the club like wildfire. Then the sight of Nat's body being carried out just hours later. And the news of Ben's demise and the missing diamonds. It was all too crazy.

Daphne had passed through the dining room yesterday when Nat and Ben were dining with Thomas Pilsner. They had looked like they were having such a good time that Daphne hoped they'd ask her to join them. But they hadn't. You win some and you lose some, she had thought at the time, trying not to be angry that they ignored her. It was obviously a boys' lunch. And what turned out to be Nat and Ben's last lunch.

Daphne had bought her apartment when she was forty and making lots of money doing voice-overs for commercials and cartoons. Through the years, she had also appeared in many off-Broadway productions, playing comic roles. Although she worked more than most actors, she still had plenty of free time to devote to sticking her nose into the affairs of the other residents and members of the Settlers' Club. She had been married once, in her twenties, to a man she had done a scene with in acting class. Unfortunately she had fallen in love with the character he played. It didn't take long to figure out he was no Rhett Butler.

Now Daphne was sixty and as energetic as ever. She had always wished to remarry, but to her disappointment it hadn't happened. She had no family to speak of, so she always said that her friends were her family, frequently inviting people into her apartment for parties and get-togethers. She even had people over to listen to her play the piano. The piano-playing parties had become the hardest draw, ever since she made the mistake of putting out a tip jar, thereby offending several of her guests. But that was done in a moment of high anxiety, when she had just lost a commercial and was afraid she'd never work again.

Still a redhead, thanks to monthly trips to a local salon, Daphne was an attractive woman with a Greenwich Village look about her. She favored berets and scarves and long skirts and lace-up boots. Daphne's bohemian, artsy sensibilities had drawn her to the Settlers' Club in the first place. After all, the club had been founded by a gentleman who had abhorred the stuffiness of other clubs in the city. He had wanted people with a sense of adventure, people who appreciated the arts. He also believed that women should be accepted as members in their own right. What better place to meet interesting people? Daphne had thought twenty years ago.

As Daphne sat in her apartment reading her favorite newspaper, the *New York World,* which featured a story about an old man who was retiring from his job as a doorman at the Plaza after more than fifty years of service, she sighed. He's seen a lot, she thought. And so have I, living on the ground floor of this joint.

She put the paper down. Time to get dressed. After all, today I am a working actress.

Daphne had managed to get a job as stand-in for one of the actresses in the film shooting at the

Settlers' Club that day. It's true it wasn't like having a real part, but at least she'd meet people in the business. And she needed to meet new people. Members of the club were dropping like flies.

She heard Thomas's voice outside in the hallway. She ran to the peephole and stole a look. He was walking by with a young woman who looked so familiar. Who was she?

"Wait a minute!" Daphne whispered. "I just saw her picture in the paper. That's Regan Reilly, and she's a private detective. Thomas must have called her in!"

"Are you sure you don't mind staying in Nat's apartment?" Thomas was asking.

Stay in his apartment! Daphne let the peephole snap shut. I don't have time now, she thought. But I'll go up there later with a tray of my cookies, and I'll offer to be of service in any way I can. I'll tell her about those meat-market parties held across the hall from Nat's that don't welcome women of a certain age!

"There is a season, turn, turn, turn," she trilled as she ran to her bedroom to get ready.

9

Regan followed Thomas off the elevator and down the red carpeted hallway to Nat's apartment. The walls were covered with framed collages of black-and-white photos capturing decades of Settlers' Club parties.

"A lot of history here," Regan said.

"One hundred years of history, Regan," Thomas said as he unlocked the heavy wooden door to Nat's apartment. It opened onto a foyer with wood paneling. To the right, Regan could see the spacious living room.

"And for the last fifty years, Nat called this apartment his home," Thomas said quietly as he led her inside.

"One of those great old apartments," Regan commented.

In the living room, Regan's eyes fixed on a tiny stained-glass window up in the corner. It gave the room the solemn feeling of an old church. "What a wonderful place to escape to," Regan said, taking it all in. "And look at these sheep."

Thomas smiled ruefully. "The story goes that Nat and his wife bought them years ago. As you look around the apartment, you'll see that Wendy had a thing for sheep. As a matter of fact, it was her expressed wish that when they both died these two sheep would have a place of honor in the front parlor. I guess I should bring them down there sooner rather than later."

"When did she die?" Regan asked.

"Three years ago. They'd been married for forty-five years."

Regan sighed. "That's tough. He must have been lonely."

"Nat didn't change a thing around here after she died. Her dressing table in the bedroom still has all her perfumes and knickknacks, just as she left them. He said he kept expecting her to come out of the bathroom and sit down at that table like she used to and brush her hair before going to bed."

"He did have good friends, though."

"The group he played cards with were his best friends."

Regan walked over to the antique desk. "This is where the jewelry was left out."

Thomas looked pained. He just nodded.

"Where is the safe?"

"Behind these books." Thomas removed several old volumes from one of the lower shelves and placed them on the desk. He then pushed the paneling aside to reveal the safe.

"That's pretty well hidden," Regan said. "My mother has a safe in the closet of her bedroom, but it's in plain view. A couple of years ago the house was burglarized and the safe was bashed in. All of her good jewelry was stolen. She always said it was safer when she hid it in a box in the attic."

Thomas nodded. "My grandmother was always hiding her jewelry, but then she could never remember where it was. After she died we had to be so careful about throwing anything out. We found jewelry hidden in secret compartments in books."

"You know, Thomas, one of the things I do want to do is make a preliminary search of the apartment to see if the diamonds are here."

"Okay, but I still say he kept them in a red box in the safe."

The doorbell rang.

"Who on earth?" Thomas asked rhetorically as he hurried to the door.

Regan waited, making a mental list of all the things she had to do to get started. And look at all these books, she thought. That red box could be hidden in any one of them.

A sound not unlike a lone dog's howl in the wilderness echoed through the apartment. Regan ran to the front door. Thomas was leaning against the wall, a small red velvet box in his hands. A fiftyish woman dressed in a maid's uniform was standing in the hallway with a sympathetic look on her face and "tsk tsks" coming from her mouth. She reminded Regan of Edith Bunker.

"What happened?" Regan asked.

"I heard all the talk this morning about the red box that was missing. Well, I found it! I knew Thomas was up here, so I ran up as fast as I could."

"It's empty!" Thomas cried.

"Where did you find it?" Regan asked.

"In the wastebasket in Thomas's office."

Regan looked at Thomas, who seemed as if he were about to sink through the floor.

10

The world headquarters of Biggest Apple Productions was based in the apartment of Stanley Stock, president, founder, and sole employee of the organization. The apartment was actually a drafty old gas station on the Lower West Side of Manhattan, but it did have a nice view of the Hudson River. Stanley had converted it into a home and office with two kitchen chairs set up in the corner for use when he interviewed studio guests for his weekly show on free-access television. Right above the set was a rack of spongy-looking tires left over from the good old days. A faint scent of gasoline still hung in the air, and there were those who said it affected Stanley's power of reason.

The station had actually belonged to Stanley's

father, and over the years, Stanley had worked there on and off. Because he hadn't inherited any of his father's mechanical ability, Stanley had spent most of his fifty-eight years working in various outside sales jobs. He'd sold everything from Fuller brushes to magazine subscriptions over the phone. An affable fellow, he didn't mind being hung up on hundreds of times a day. He'd just dial the next number and go into his spiel until he heard the click in his ear. His coworkers always liked Stanley and usually ended up telling him their problems. Stanley always took their side, agreeing with everything they said.

"Right," he'd say emphatically as they stood around the water cooler or coffee machine. "You're so right!" Every conversation usually included a "That's terrible."

After his father's funeral a year ago, Stanley decided that he had had enough. He'd quit his latest job, which he must have had for at least a month, and ceremoniously closed the garage doors of his inheritance to the broken down cars of the world, and moved in. He considered it to be a pretty hip move, the first hip move he'd made in his life. Other people in downtown New York lived in trendy lofts that had formerly been warehouses. What's wrong with a gas station?

The question that hung in the petrol-smelling

air was, Now what? What do I do with the rest of my life? Stanley asked himself over and over. He had enough money to get by, but he still felt he hadn't made his mark on the world. He was certainly right about that.

Stanley discovered something that up till now had been totally unfamiliar to him. Ambition. It awakened in his soul when he finally discovered his true calling.

At night he'd lay his portly body on the slip-covered couch and aim his remote control at the television that he'd rigged to the lift that formerly raised sickly cars into the air. But no matter what was on, he'd always find himself switching back to the shows on Free-Speech television. It was a cable station that by law had to be made available to anyone who wanted access. As a result, many programs made their way onto the air that were astonishingly bad, with their poor production values, lame content, and wacky hosts. So bad they made you stop and look, like the scene of an accident.

Stanley found them entertaining.

"I can do better than that," he finally cried. "I must go on the air!"

Armed with a video camera, he had hit the streets of New York. People took to him, just as his coworkers had. Everyone he interviewed told him their hard luck stories. I should have been a shrink, he often thought. Before long he had a segment called "Gripe du jour" that became very popular. There was no end to the number of people willing to stand in front of the camera and vent.

"The idiot at the deli handed me my coffee in a soggy brown bag and to make matters worse, the lid wasn't on properly. The bag broke and the coffee went all over my coat," someone screamed to him the other day. "I hate that!"

Finally, even Stanley had had enough. He thought of starting a show on healing but soon realized there were too many of those already. Then, walking home last week with a camera full of taped gripes, including those of a bunch of tourists in Times Square who did nothing but complain about the subways, Stanley was truly dispirited. He reached his front door, unlocked it, and gratefully walked inside.

He sauntered past the candy machines and put his camera bag down on the all-purpose table. Shuffling through his mail, he dropped the junk letters onto the table one at a time. The last envelope in his hand looked somewhat interesting. He had ripped it open and read the letter from Maldwin Feckles, heralding the beginning of his butler school. Hmmmm, Stanley had thought as he read. Maybe I can turn this into something interesting.

And he had. Just last night, he had filmed the student butlers at work at the Princess of Love's party for quality singles. He was sorry that the party had ended so soon, after all hell had broken loose across the hall. He'd have to incorporate what happened into his story. Somehow.

Now, as Stanley sat drinking his second cup of morning coffee, he reflected on the fact that if he was going to cover the Settlers' Club's big party tomorrow night, if he was going to include it in his piece, then he should really go up and take some footage of Gramercy Park to use in his introduction. I'll head up there and interview the man on the street, he thought. Maybe the butlers will be around and I can have them stroll around the park.

He took the tape from last night out of his video camera and reloaded. In a half-hour, Stanley was headed uptown.

11

I'm sorry," the maid was saying. "I was only trying to help." She turned to Regan and stared at her as if to say, Now what are you going to do?

"Are you all right, Thomas?" Regan asked as he clenched the red box that was stamped PEM-ROD JEWELERS.

"Regan, tell me this is a nightmare."

"I'll agree with you on that."

"Regan!"

"Sorry, Thomas. You look white as a ghost. Maybe you should sit down."

Back into the living room they went, the maid, Clara, close at their heels.

"I don't think I'm up to going back in Nat's bathroom right now. Clara, will you show Regan the rest of the apartment?"

"Of course," Clara said with a bright smile. "Come this way. I used to clean Mr. Pemrod's apartment every week. What a nice man. It's a shame he's passed over."

Regan nodded. "Thomas, just relax here for a minute."

"Regan," he said quickly. "I'm having a panic attack. I think I'd be more comfortable in my office. Would you meet me there when you're finished?"

Thomas, don't lose it, Regan thought. She felt a sudden rush of affection for him. He looked like a deer caught in headlights. "Of course. Go ahead," she said. "I'm sure Clara will be very helpful."

Clara beamed. "You know, being somebody's maid means you get to know a lot about a person. Have I taken care of some slobs in my day. But Nat, he was pretty good. Ya know, sometimes he . . ."

"Hold that thought," Regan said as she escorted Thomas to the door. "See you in a few minutes." She took the red box from his hands and turned back to Clara who was clearly enjoying the drama.

"You were saying . . . ?" Regan prodded.

"Oh, yeah, I had one couple. Always left a mess. Disgusting—"

"I mean about Nat," Regan interrupted as gently as she could.

"Oh, yeah, Nat." Clara raised both her hands and looked up to the ceiling as though she'd find some insight there. "So sad after his wife died. She had a thing for all these crazy sheep." Clara started walking down the hallway toward the master bedroom. At the doorway she stood aside to allow Regan to step in front of her. "Pretty, isn't it?"

"Yes." Regan noticed the dressing table that Thomas had mentioned, with all of Wendy's toiletries still there. "Oh, and there is the bathroom," she said, inching closer. Regan took a deep breath. In the absolute quiet, her senses were heightened, alert to catch every detail of this scene of death.

"I have the worst time keeping that marble clean," Clara said plaintively. "I've tried all sorts of cleaners. But none of them was that great . . ."

It's funny what people feel the need to talk about at times like this, Regan thought. But I know she means well. "That's a big Jacuzzi to scrub," she said in sympathy.

"Yeah," Clara said. "But I've hardly had to touch it since Wendy died."

"How come?" Regan asked.

"Because Nat hated baths. He only took showers."

12

Thomas, now try to think happy thoughts."

Thomas's girlfriend, Janey, clad as ever in a cardigan sweater, straight skirt, sensible shoes, her outfit pulled together by her most cherished possession, a single strand of pearls, was doing her best to comfort her agitated boyfriend. They were in his office. She was standing behind him, massaging his temples.

"How could everything have gone wrong so fast?" he asked, his voice quivering. "We had so many plans for the club. Tea dances, brunches, ballroom dances, lectures, culture . . ."

"It's not all over. And the brunch you had last Sunday was very successful," Janey said as her fingers now disappeared into Thomas's bushy hair and kneaded his scalp.

"Not really," he whined. "When that group of college kids left, I heard one of them say he'd seen younger faces on cash."

Janey shook her head from side to side. "We shouldn't have invited kids on spring break. A gracious brunch is not what they were looking for. But everyone else enjoyed it."

"The only two who didn't complain about the food were Nat and Ben, and now they're both dead."

Janey sighed. "They were the two nicest people in the club."

Thomas reached up and took Janey's hands in his. "How do you think that red box ended up in my wastebasket?"

Janey came around and sat, very ladylike, on the edge of Thomas's desk. "Someone threw it there," she said with steely resolve. "Someone who was on these premises yesterday and stole the diamonds."

"But who?" Thomas cried.

A knock on the door caused them both to jump.

"Yes, come in," Thomas called as he sat up straight.

When the door opened, he saw that it was Regan Reilly.

"I hope I'm not interrupting anything."

"No, no," Thomas insisted. "Regan, this is my girlfriend, Janey."

"Hello, Janey." Regan extended her hand.

"Hello." Janey's response was meek.

"Thomas, we have a lot of things to discuss," Regan said.

Janey glanced down at her watch. "I'd better run."

"You can stay," Thomas said in an almost pleading tone.

"No, sweetness, I've got to get to work." Janey grabbed her beige coat off the chair. It seemed to Regan that everything about her was beige. "I'll see you both later."

"She's very nice," Regan remarked when she and Thomas were alone.

"She is simply wonderful. The most wonderful woman that ever lived," Thomas insisted.

How do you know? Regan thought, but asked, "Where does she work?"

"At home. She has a business cooking meals for people too busy to cook for themselves. People order up to a week's worth of meals and then store them in the freezer. She's so wonderful, she gives a discount to the elderly. And on top of that, she's the biggest good-deed doer I've ever met."

"That's wonderful," Regan found herself saying, thinking of a girl who lived down the hall from her in college who was always going around collecting money for some good cause or other. Regan spotted her years later at an airport with a shaved head, a fixed grin, and the same tin cup ready for donations. But Regan had to hand it to her. She was committed. Janey seemed like the same type.

"Regan!" Thomas suddenly blurted. "I have nothing to do with that red box being in my garbage."

"I believe you," Regan said simply. "But it makes it pretty clear that someone took those diamonds. I think the whole thing was well planned. Including Nat's death." She filled him in on what the maid had told her.

Thomas cocked his head. "I can't imagine someone not liking baths."

Inwardly, Regan groaned. "But if he didn't, whatever the reason, it makes his death much more suspect. And it makes me question whether Ben had a heart attack because someone actually pushed him in front of that bus."

"A murder in the club! It's never happened before."

"And I want to do my part in making sure it doesn't happen again, Thomas. I have to talk to the woman across the hall who had the party."

"The Princess of Love."

"Whatever."

"Right away." Thomas picked up the phone and a few minutes later they were knocking on her door.

"Are you a quality single?" Lydia inquired with a big smile when Thomas introduced them.

"It depends on who you ask," Regan answered.

Lydia laughed as though that was the funniest thing she had ever heard. Regan smiled in spite of herself. People who laugh at your jokes certainly do gain extra points, she thought.

"Well, come in," Lydia said, stretching out her expensively bangled arm. With her jewelry and makeup and sexy lounging outfit, she looked as though she were about to pose for the cover of a romance novel.

Makes sense, Regan thought. She dresses for the job.

Thomas turned to Regan. "Your bags are still out by the front desk. I'll bring them upstairs. Here's the key to the apartment."

Regan looked at her watch. "After I talk to Lydia, I'll go in and call Nat's brother."

"I'll be in my office," Thomas said, and like a shot, he was gone.

Regan followed Lydia inside. The apartment was architecturally a mirror image of Nat's, but the resemblance ended there. The living room contained six pastel love seats. No couches. No chairs. Just love seats. Pale pink carpeting covered the floor, and large murals of blooming floral arrangements brightened the walls.

"I like a happy feeling in a home," Lydia explained, following Regan's glance around the room.

"Very nice," Regan said, thinking that the decor was oddly interesting. "I see you like love seats."

"My singles parties are much more successful since I bought the love seats. People are forced to sit closer to each other. It either turns them off or on. Either way, you find out fast if there's interest. It's a big time-saver."

"And what no one seems to have enough of is time," Regan said as she took out her notebook.

"Look at Nat. His time is up. He's on a different plane now. But he's happier," Lydia pronounced.

"How do you know?" Regan asked.

"I just have a feeling. I'm a little psychic, you know. He's reunited with his great love, Wendy, and that's what's most important. And he didn't suffer."

Once again Regan asked, "How do you know?"

"If he slipped in the tub and hit his head, it was over fast. He didn't have a long illness."

"But he could have had several more good years," Regan said. "He was full of plans."

Lydia sighed. "He did seem to enjoy life. I didn't know him all that well. I just moved in here last fall. My first party here was held on Valentine's Day, and I invited him in, even though he's way over my target age group. I wanted to be neighborly. He loved to tell jokes. They weren't always the best jokes, but he was fun."

"Did he come to any other parties?"

"Sometimes he'd knock on the door and just stay for a few minutes. Usually because he had a new joke to tell."

Regan decided to get to the point. "Lydia, do you think I could get a list of who was at the party last night?"

Lydia looked aghast. "I know there are supposedly diamonds missing. But if you go questioning my guests, you'll ruin my business."

"What did you hear about the diamonds?" Regan asked.

"My butler, Maldwin, told me that he'd heard there was going to be a big announcement about Nat and his friend Ben donating the money from some diamonds they owned and were planning to sell. The announcement was planned for the anniversary party on Saturday night. We were both so happy. Regan, we want this club to stay open. We've set up our businesses here."

"And other people knew too?"

"Well, people were talking about it at the party."

"Who?"

"There was a cameraman here who's doing a story on us and the club. He had heard the news and was asking people if they might want to join the club now that it was going to get a lot of money. It was all done in fun. Everyone was in a good mood."

"Then it's in both of our best interests to get those diamonds back, Lydia."

"I know but . . ."

"Lydia, all I want to do is talk to the people who were here. They won't think they're suspects. I just want to see if they saw anything or heard anything. Believe me, most innocent people love to be involved in investigations. They think it's exciting."

Lydia cocked her head. "But a lot of people don't want others to know they go to singles events. They get embarrassed."

"Who's going to find out? Besides, do you want to live across the hall from where a crime may have taken place and have it go unsolved? Or worse yet, have someone coming to your parties who is a criminal?"

Lydia sat up straight. "Of course not."

"I'm here to help Thomas get this straightened out. He could lose his job over this. He told me that he made a deal with you to let you have these parties and the butler classes in this apartment. If he goes, I doubt you'll find another manager who is so agreeable. And if this place closes down, you're really out of luck."

Lydia stared at her long, red fingernails. Finally she looked up. "Regan, I believe that everyone has a soul mate out there. It is my journey in life to help people find that special someone . . ."

Oh, brother, Regan thought. As long as they pay you.

"I invite people into my home to open their hearts. To open their souls. To allow a little love and light into their consciousness, which was dark, dark, dark . . ."

"The list, Lydia?"

"I was getting to that." Lydia cleared her throat. "Because confidentiality is a big part of my business—you know people like to tell stories about how they met their soul mate on a crowded train . . . it's rarely true. Anyway, what I am willing to do is invite everyone back here tonight. It'll be a free party. I'll tell them it's because of all the excitement last night. You can talk to them at the party. It won't seem so much like you think one of them is guilty."

"Will people be available to come on such short notice?"

"If it's free, believe me they'll come. At least for a drink."

"What if someone can't make it?"

"Then I'll give you their name."

Regan stood up. "All right, Lydia. Tonight then. I understand your butler had his students serving at the party. Can you arrange for them to all be here as well?"

Lydia jumped up from the couch and stretched out her arms. "We'll re-create the evening."

"Let's hope it's not a complete reenactment."

Lydia laughed merrily.

"I'll be in and out today. Let me know how many of the group you can round up."

Lydia wiggled her fingers. "I'm ready to start dialing for dates."

13

Georgette Hughes and Blaise Bowden sat in glum silence as they sipped their morning coffee at the tiny table in their dingy rented room on the Upper West Side of Manhattan.

"I'm sorry!" she blurted.

"I didn't say anything," he growled.

On display in front of them were the four glass stones that Nat had removed from Dolly and Bah-Bah's eye sockets.

"I can't understand it," Georgette whined. She was a short, ample-bosomed woman with long brown hair streaked with blond highlights who had a penchant for strong-smelling perfume and big earrings. Her brown eyes could display warmth, but her face could turn wicked in an instant. "I saw the diamonds the other night.

When I rang the bell, Nat was surprised to see me. He had all the jewelry out. I'm telling you, the four diamonds were there."

Blaise picked up the four glass stones and threw them on the floor. "You could buy these in the five-and-ten." He was a large man, tall, sandy-haired, attractive and smooth, yet underneath it all, not as sly as Georgette. Georgette's sister had dubbed him "the cardboard box." But for Georgette he was the perfect match. They were partners in crime. Drifters. Opportunists. Two con artists who'd been together for six years, ripping people off all over the country. "I'm stuck in that idiotic butler class for another couple of weeks. I hate it."

"Do you think those singles parties I go to faithfully are any treat? How many more times can I stand that horrible small talk? And how about all the time I spent wooing old Nat? He was a nice man, but he didn't exactly ring my bell. And now he's dead and I've got nothing to show for it."

Blaise stood up. "Look at this dingy dump. We haven't had a score in so long it's pathetic. You should have taken some of his wife's jewelry."

"I thought I had four diamonds worth millions, and besides, I happened to be carrying a very small purse. I went in to his apartment when I heard the gossip about him selling the diamonds. I was frantic. Did I know that last night was the night I'd have to grab them? If I had, I'd have carried a bigger purse, I'll tell you that right now."

"Well, what are we going to do?"

"For right now, you go to butler class. If you manage to graduate, that's going to come in handy. You'll have access to all those grand homes that are just aching to be robbed."

"I can't take all the pressure. And I can't stand any more of Maldwin Feckles's endless preaching about butlering hints and tips and do's and don't's. 'A butler should be eager to serve.' 'A butler should display good breeding.'" Blaise's voice rose as he continued. "'A butler should always greet his employer with the proper respect.' 'A butler shouldn't question any requests.' I want to yell *Shut up!*"

"Please, Blaise, you're giving me a headache."

"And I hate it when you go on dates with other guys."

"Don't get me started," Georgette protested. "You think I like it, going out with those losers to see if they have anything worth stealing? And if I didn't accept any dates, Lydia wouldn't keep on inviting me to her parties. That was the only way I got to sneak over and see Nat. I should have hit him over the head and taken the diamonds the first time I saw them instead of planning to replace them with fakes."

"Don't even joke about hitting him over the head. It looks like someone did."

"You don't have to tell me. I was there. When I heard the back door open, I nearly died. I ran out of there as fast as I could. And you have the nerve to ask me why I didn't grab his dead wife's jewelry."

"You could be charged with murder."

"Blaise! Stop it! I didn't do anything to hurt him."

"We've got to get back in that apartment and look for the diamonds. They must be in there."

"Well, I can't go back there until tomorrow night—for the club party. Lydia's next soirée isn't till next week. You take the key. If you can get in there today, do it!" Georgette stood up and put her arms around her lover.

"You smell good," he said as he buried his face in her neck.

Georgette stroked the back of his neck. "We'll get those diamonds, you'll graduate, and then we'll go on a nice vacation."

Blaise laughed. "Where I won't have to polish the silver."

"No, honey, your job is to *steal* the silver."

They embraced, and then Georgette watched as Blaise put on his coat and gloves and headed out the door to butler school.

14

When he formed his butler school, Maldwin
Feckles had decided that field trips would be an
important part of his students' education. There
were cigar stores to visit, china shops, designer-
clothing showrooms, wine shops, jewelry stores—
so many places to go and learn about the finest
things money can buy. And of course how to use
and care for them properly.

Now Maldwin stood with his first class of four
students in a crowded, dark, and dusty antiques
shop in rural New Jersey. He had hoped to
acquaint them with objects that are found in
homes that reeked of old money. He also wanted
to pick up a few serving pieces for Lydia's future
parties. Last night three of her good plates had

fallen off the kitchen counter and smashed to smithereens on the floor.

No one had taken the blame, of course, but Maldwin had tried to take it in stride. It had been right after one of the guests came running in to say there was a dead body across the hall.

Maldwin sniffed as he glanced around the shop, which turned out to offer mostly a hodge-podge of other people's junk. But after careful exploration, with Maldwin picking up objects such as silver trays and odd-shaped forks and pointing out their usefulness, he had managed to find several items for purchase that he would put into service at Miss Lydia's apartment. One was a silver soup tureen with a tarnish buildup that must have taken decades, another was a set of espresso spoons that one of his students thought was for babies, and three were stained teapots that would require scrubbing with industrial strength denture cleanser.

They were now being packaged by the clerk, who seemed to think that everything in the shop was some sort of treasure.

"Students," Maldwin said, pointing to a stack of china dishes. "These should never be stored without a protective pad between each plate. The pad can be made of bubble wrap, if need be, but the plates will scratch each other if they're not—"

Maldwin's cell phone rang.

Thank God, Blaise thought.

"I thought you said cell phones were rude," Vinnie Checkers mumbled. He was clearly the troublemaker student. Maldwin wasn't sure why he had even signed up for the class. He looked like an extra from *Grease*.

"They are rude when they disrupt meals, entertainment, or if the cell phone user insists on carrying on his business in a loud voice on trains, buses, and in other public areas." Maldwin sniffed as he pulled the phone out of his breast pocket. "Otherwise, they are most handy . . . hello . . . what? . . . oh my . . . another party tonight . . . we will return to the city at once . . . it should take a couple of hours." He hung up the phone as fear seized his stomach and began a slow gnaw.

"What's the matter, Maldwin?" Albert Ketler asked, his mouth hanging open in a most unbecoming fashion. It had occurred to Maldwin that he had a constantly befuddled look about him. Another one who was only accepted because the school is just getting started, Maldwin thought.

"We are returning to the city. Miss Lydia is having another party this evening."

"Another party?" Vinnie asked. "I thought we were getting out early today."

"You knew when you signed up for this course

that it would be intensive. And flexibility is an important part of any butler's life. You have to be ready at a moment's notice to go with the flow, as they say," Maldwin said as the clerk came back with the packages.

"We're getting in some good pieces next week," he said, peering owlishly through his glasses as he handed Maldwin his credit card and receipt. "Be sure to come back."

"Serving plates are what I need." Maldwin handed him his card. "If you get any good ones, let me know."

"Everybody breaks them."

"Tell me about it." Maldwin turned to his assembled group. He raised the walking stick that he always carried on his excursions. "Follow me!" He led them out to the thirty-year-old Vista Cruiser station wagon that Lydia had had since she was a teenager.

"It's the one part of my old life that I don't want to give up," she'd told Maldwin.

Vinnie opened the back door and climbed into the third row of seats, with Albert close behind him. The two had bonded quickly in the first week of class and wanted to sit as far away as possible from the teacher. It had been a late night last night, an early morning this morning, and they were both hungry and tired. And now it would be another late night. They were both hoping for a little nap time in the car.

No such luck.

Little Harriet, the only girl in the group, had jumped in the front seat with Feckles.

"Can we listen to the etiquette tape on the way back?" she asked hopefully.

Vinnie and Albert groaned as Blaise Bowden, the quiet loner, took a seat by himself in the second row.

"Of course we will," Maldwin said as the station wagon bounced out of the bumpy driveway and past a big WELCOME sign. "But first we will go over all the mistakes you made last night. Vinnie," he called, "how could you improve your performance of last night?"

"You mean after the party?"

Maldwin winced as Vinnie and Albert chuckled.

"No, I mean in your role as butler."

Vinnie frowned. "I think I did pretty good last night."

Harriet turned around and looked at him. "You're not supposed to put ice cubes in red wine."

"Don't insult my mother!" Vinnie said. "She liked her red wine nice and cold."

"Now, now," Maldwin said. "We don't ever want

to insult anyone. That is not what a true gentleman or lady does. And many things are a matter of taste. But perhaps it was sangria that was your mother's beverage? Sangria is best served chilled."

"All I know is there was fruit in the bowl."

Maldwin nodded. "Yes, Vinnie. That would have been sangria. When you are serving fine red wines, they are best served room temperature."

Vinnie waved his hand at him. "I've got a headache."

"Perhaps we could use some quiet time," Maldwin agreed. And a Rolaid, he thought. "I'll put in the etiquette tape. But first, does anyone have a helpful hint of the day?"

"A true gentleman or lady never jangles the change in their pockets," Harriet blurted.

"Very good!" Maldwin cried. "Harriet, this all comes to you naturally."

She nodded enthusiastically. "It annoys the hell out of people."

Maldwin blinked, quickly shoved the cassette into the tape player, and tried to put out of his mind the sense that everything felt doomed.

15

Regan took a look down the hallway before unlocking the door to Nat's apartment. Opposite the elevator at the end of the hallway was a steel door. High time to check that out, she thought as she walked down and opened it.

A small square area of gray metal and cement greeted her. A gray service elevator stood like a fortress a few feet in front of her. On the wall to her right was a metal door, on the wall to her left was a metal door, and just next to it was a staircase that went down. The air smelled dank. Two garbage cans for paper and plastic recyclables were positioned next to the elevator.

It didn't take long for Regan to realize that the two doors were the service entrances to Nat's and Lydia's apartments. She had seen Nat's from the inside when Clara gave her a quick tour of his apartment.

So if anyone wanted to sneak into Nat's apartment without being seen, this would be the better choice, Regan thought. Could someone have had a key?

Regan inserted the key she was holding in Nat's back door. To her astonishment, it worked. The same key for the front and back doors? she thought. That's unusual. She pushed the door open, stepped inside, and found herself in the little hallway just off the back of the kitchen. She locked the door. The apartment was still, except for the humming of the refrigerator.

Regan sighed. The kitchen was narrow and long, with cream-colored cabinets and appliances. Some of the cabinet doors were inlaid with glass, through which old-fashioned cups, saucers, and plates could be seen neatly stacked in rows. The room itself was old-fashioned and cozy, but seemed isolated from the rest of the apartment. It must hark back to the days when people who had these apartments didn't spend much time in the kitchen. But their help did.

There was no table in the room. The only concession to modern-day eat-in-the-kitchen living was two stools at the countertop opposite the sink. A swinging door opened onto another little foyer just off the dining room, and a swinging door at the other end led to the hallway down to the bedrooms and the living room.

Did Nat spend much time in here? Regan wondered. Was he futzing around the kitchen yesterday at this time? It certainly looked neat and clean. Clara said she had cleaned the apartment on Tuesday. Today was Friday.

What about Nat's dinner last night? Regan wondered. She opened the cabinet under the sink and pulled out the lined plastic garbage can. Coffee grounds, orange peels, cookie wrappers, and a paper plate were right on top. Regan lifted the paper plate and underneath it were several pigs in blankets.

Hors d'oeuvres.

What you'd serve at a party.

Not something you'd prepare for just yourself.

Oh God, Regan thought. I must remember to check out the menu at Lydia's get-together this evening. She rifled through the rest of the garbage and found eggshells, an empty vitamin bottle, and an empty men's cologne bottle. Most people put on their cologne in the bedroom, Regan mused.

Regan shoved the can back under the sink and decided she desperately needed a cup of tea. She filled the kettle, then carefully reached in a cabinet for a cup and saucer. She located teabags in one of the ceramic canisters that had paintings of sheep on them. In the refrigerator was a carton of skim milk. It was the same brand she'd used that morning in her parents' apartment. Somehow it seemed longer ago than that. I wonder how the crime convention is going, she thought. I would love to catch some of it.

Her hot tea in hand, she sat down at the counter in the kitchen and picked up the phone. She dialed the number of Nat's brother in Palm Springs, California. A feeble voice answered at the other end.

Regan identified herself.

"Oh, hello, Regan. Carl Pemrod here." The voice sounded a little more chipper.

"I'm so sorry about your brother," Regan said.

"Me too. We weren't that close, but he was blood. I didn't grow up with him. He was my half brother."

"Oh, he was."

"Yes. My mother wasn't too thrilled with our father after he left. So we didn't have much contact with his second family."

"I understand Nat didn't have any other brothers and sisters."

"Not that I know of."

"As you know, I'm conducting an investigation—"

"About how he slipped in the tub? It happens a lot, you know. I broke my hip last year. Terrible thing, getting old."

"It is," Regan agreed. "Did you know anything about these diamonds he had?"

"Nope. Like I told ya, we didn't have much contact."

"Do you know Nat's lawyer?"

"Nope. Like I told ya . . ."

"Right," Regan said. "Well, Mr. Pemrod, first of all I want to thank you for allowing me access to the apartment here."

"Oh, sure. Listen, Regan, it's no problem. I know Nat wanted to leave everything to that club of his. He was always so proud of that place. Whenever I talked to him, that's all he talked about. The club this, the club that. Truth to tell, sometimes I put my ear on automatic pilot when he went on about it. The members were his family, really."

"I'm glad he was happy here."

"I think he was."

"Well, I'll only be staying for a couple of days. I live in California, too, and I have to get back."

"If you come to Palm Springs, drop by."

"Well, thank you."

"I met your mother at the library. Nice lady."

"Thank you," Regan said again. "I'll keep you

posted on what happens here. I understand you want Nat's body to be cremated."

"Cemeteries are getting too full. We all should be cremated."

"Yes, well, apparently that was Nat's wish as well."

"Wendy was cremated. Nat took her ashes back to the countryside where she grew up, in England. Some of my friends have had their ashes thrown off cruise ships."

"Uh-huh," Regan mumbled. "Well, I have a lot to look into here, but as I said, I'll keep you posted."

"That's nice of you."

"Well, you are Nat's brother. And again, thank you for letting me stay here. In the next couple of days I hope to talk to his lawyer and get his affairs in order. We'll get everything straightened out," Regan promised in an optimistic tone that did not reflect her real feelings.

"Okay. If he left anything to his older brother, Carl, so much the better. Now I'm going out by the pool. It's ninety degrees here today. What's it like there?" Carl asked in a teasing tone.

"About sixty degrees cooler."

Carl chuckled. "I always told Nat he was crazy to live in New York."

16

Georgette had a bad morning. Here it was Friday, March 12th, and she'd wasted all her time since Valentine's Day on Nat Pemrod. She was sure that he had fallen for her. That he was just about to give her presents and money. When she'd gotten him tipsy the other night, he'd spilled the beans about the diamonds. He'd even told her he liked to have fun with them. Whatever that meant. But before she had a chance to go out and buy cubic zirconiums to substitute for them, someone else had already moved in for the kill.

Who was it? Somebody else had to have taken the diamonds, and Georgette was bound and determined to find out who it was. She hadn't been a con artist for ten years for nothing. She and Blaise were usually so good at this game.

They just seemed to be down on their luck lately.

Or there was always the chance that Nat had hidden the diamonds somewhere in the apartment. Is that what he meant by playing games? God knows she'd listened to all his stories about the practical jokes he'd played over the years.

She went into a fast-food restaurant on Broadway, purchased a cup of coffee, and looked around. An old man was hunched over a newspaper in a corner booth. Georgette sashayed over and cleared her throat.

"Excuse me, is this seat taken?" she asked, pointing to the orange plastic bench that was nailed to the floor.

He looked up at her, smiled slightly, and motioned for her to sit down. He was bald, with a large round face, smooth clear skin, and watery blue eyes. His clothes looked like they had seen better days, but he was wearing a shirt and tie. From the corner of her eye, Georgette could see that he was sporting a pair of thick-soled white sneakers.

A perfect target, she thought. Surely he has a few shekels that he can do without.

"Sit down, my beauty," he insisted.

This is better than I thought, Georgette mused. "Thank you, sir," she said.

"What's a lovely girl like you doing all alone?"

Georgette batted her eyes as she sat on the impossibly uncomfortable bench. "I just moved into town, and I don't know many people yet." She leaned in so he could smell her perfume.

He sneezed, waved his hands, and pulled a handkerchief out of his pocket. "Sit back, my beauty. Sit back. Your perfume isn't good for my throat."

"Your throat?"

"I was a singer in my day. Performed everywhere. Now I was thinking, if you give me a few hundred bucks a week, I'll teach you to sing and have you on Broadway in five years. I can still hit middle C, you know." He opened his mouth and belted out several notes as Georgette jumped up and ran out of the restaurant. On her way, she heard one of the busboys yell, "Cool it, Mr. C. We told you no singing in here."

Out on the street, Georgette struggled to regain her composure. My planets must not be in alignment, she thought. Just then her cell phone rang. Let it be Blaise, she thought.

"Hello . . . oh Lydia, what a surprise . . . Another party tonight?" Georgette's pulse quickened. "How nice of you . . . Is there anything I can do to help? I'm actually off today . . . No? . . . Well, maybe I'll get there early . . . I'd love to talk to Maldwin about signing up for his next butler class . . . Yes, really . . . Okay, see you later."

Georgette put the phone back in her purse and breathed a sigh of relief. Maybe I can get back in Nat's apartment tonight, she thought. As she hurried down the block, she passed a coffee shop. Stopping in her tracks, she turned around and went back. You never know, she thought, as she opened the door and made a beeline for the seat next to an old man at the counter. My work is never done.

17

After Regan spoke to Carl, she took a little walk through the apartment. She found herself back in Nat's bathroom. No doubt—it was luxurious. The marble walls and floor, gleaming glass shower door, and beautiful porcelain sinks all gave the feeling of well-cared-for opulence. An electric heated towel rack stood against the wall near the Jacuzzi. One large white towel was draped over it. I bet that's the one Nat would have used last night, she thought.

Regan turned and walked over to the two hand towels that were hanging on a rack between the sinks. She hadn't really noticed them before, but now she could see that the miniature appliqués lining their borders were little sheep. My God, they had sheep everything, she thought. They're cute, but they don't look like the kind of towels that you use. They're more for show.

There was an empty towel rack on the wall next to the shower. For some reason, it seemed odd to her that it was empty. Just then something on the floor caught her eye. She walked over and picked it up. It was a tiny sheep appliqué. This must have fallen off a towel, she thought. But where's the towel?

There was no hamper in the bathroom. Regan walked into Nat's bedroom and opened the closet door. All women's clothes. These must have been Wendy's, Regan thought. She shut the door.

In the guest room, she found her suitcase on the floor and hanging bag laid out on the bed. She opened the first of two closet doors. This was obviously where Nat kept his clothes. She lifted the lid of a wicker hamper, but there were no towels in there. Just a couple of men's shirts, socks, and underwear.

Regan smiled. Even though Wendy had been dead for three years, he hadn't moved her clothes. He still had to go into the guest room to get his things. One of Regan's friends had gotten married and moved into her husband's apartment. He was so persnickety he made her use the guest bathroom and second bedroom closet. Needless to say, the marriage hadn't lasted. But Nat obviously had been devoted to his wife. And all these sheep might have driven another man crazy.

It was as if Regan were getting a feel for Nat Pemrod. I wonder if he slept in here at all. Just as Regan was pondering all this, her cell phone rang. From the Caller ID she could tell it was Jack.

"Hi there," she said.

"Regan, how's it going?"

"Let's just say it's interesting."

"I'm at the office. It's been pretty hectic, but I talked to a guy named Ronald Brier down at the 13th. He was there last night. He suggested you drop by and talk to him."

Regan looked at her watch. It was just about noon. "I think I'll head down there right now."

"And one other thing."

"What?"

"Think about where you want to have dinner on Sunday night. I'll call you later."

"Okay." Regan hung up and sat on the bed. She picked up one of the framed pictures on the bedside table. It was an old black-and-white picture of four men playing cards. This must be the Suits, she thought. Regan put it down and glanced at the other photos. They were mostly pictures of a couple at various stages of life. In one of them they were standing in a field, surrounded by sheep.

Regan pulled open the drawer of the table. A notepad and pen had been neatly placed in there.

She lifted out the pad and opened it up. The page was dated Thursday, March 11th. Yesterday!

Regan began to read and was astonished by the words in front of her.

> My little Buttercup,
>   These last four weeks have been undeniably joyous. After my dear wife, Wendy, went off to the Lord, her shepherd, I never thought I could feel anything deep for another woman. I guess I was right. While I enjoy your company, I don't think it's right to keep sneaking around with you.
>   I've decided that the rest of my life should be spent doing good for others. Who knows how long I have left?
>   They say that if you find one true love in your life then you're blessed. I figure I'll quit while I'm ahead.
>   Best of luck!
>   Natty Boy

Regan couldn't believe her eyes. Natty Boy! And who in God's name is Buttercup? More than ever, Regan felt certain that Nat's death was no accident.

18

C areful! Please be careful!" Thomas urged the men who were carrying all the film equipment into the front parlor of the club. "Don't bang into anything, please."

He was largely ignored. As anyone who's spent time on a movie set knows, the crew go about their business, unimpressed by celebrity, surroundings, or gawkers. They simply do their work.

In contrast, Thomas was running around trying to make order out of something he could not. Hollywood had arrived, and time was precious. They had one afternoon to film an important scene.

Thomas suddenly wondered if he had gotten in over his head. Outside on the narrow street, the movie trucks were taking up a lot of space. Production assistants were trying to direct traffic around the park. Electric cables were strewn all over the sidewalk.

Thomas looked out the bay window and saw people staring into the front parlor of the club. Oh dear, he thought. Sometimes things can seem like such a good idea in the planning, but then when they come to pass, your palms start to sweat. Especially now. He wanted the Settlers' Club to gain attention. But only in the right ways.

"Could you move, please?" a burly fellow holding a large piece of lighting equipment asked Thomas in a tone that barely masked his impatience.

Thomas stepped back quickly. "Of course." What can I do? What can I do? he thought. I know! I'll bring the sheep down. Wendy wanted them here, and it might be a nice touch for the movie.

Ten minutes later, with the help of Regan, who was on her way out, they brought the two sheep into the parlor and plopped them down on either side of the fireplace.

"Excuse me!" An efficient-looking thirtyish guy wearing a cap and carrying a clipboard rushed over to them. "What are you doing to the set?"

"These sheep are important to our club," Thomas said. "We thought you might want them for the movie."

"All the casting has been completed. Could you please remove them?"

Regan looked at Thomas. "Why don't we carry the sheep into your office? We'll bring them back out when they're finished filming."

"I just wanted to do the right thing by Wendy and Nat."

"I understand," Regan said. "But let's move them."

Regan had Dolly and Thomas had Bah-Bah in their arms when from behind them someone yelled, "Stop!"

They turned to see a wiry man dressed in black, sporting a black beret, and carrying an empty cigarette holder, coming toward them from the doorway. "I like the sheep. Put them back."

Regan and Thomas both shrugged and put the sheep down.

"I'm Jacques Harlow, the director of *We Must Be Dreaming.*"

"And I'm the president of the club, Thomas Pilsner, and this is my friend Regan Reilly."

"Nice."

"I'm pleased you chose to use the club for a scene in your film."

Jacques bit on the edge of the cigarette holder and spoke through his teeth. "I like the vibes here. I don't work with a script. My actors all improvise their lines. I think that a setting such as this inspires our deepest hopes and our darkest fears."

Does it ever, Regan thought.

"Would you like to be an extra?" he asked Regan with a touch of a leer.

"No," Regan answered quickly, then added, "I'm pretty busy." She turned to Thomas. "I'm heading out."

"Come to my office for a moment, Regan."

They excused themselves, stepped around the piled-up equipment, and went into Thomas's office down the hall, shutting the door behind them.

"That guy is weird," Thomas said.

"Thomas, what kind of movie is it?"

"The location manager told me it was a period piece."

"What period?"

Thomas's lip quivered. "I didn't ask. I assumed he meant Victorian."

The phone on the desk rang. Thomas picked it up and identified himself.

"The *New York World?* . . . Yes, there is a movie shooting here . . . He what? . . . Just got out of jail . . . he trashed a location in New Jersey? . . . I can't talk now . . . Good-bye." Thomas dropped the phone back in its cradle.

"I hate to ask," Regan said.

"Jacques Harlow is a nut case. He trashed a bowling alley in New Jersey where they were shooting a scene last week. He thinks he's one of the Sopranos. They just released him from jail."

Regan grimaced. "Well, somebody's paying for this film to be made. I wonder who?"

"I think it's low budget," Thomas said in a tiny voice. "We were desperate for new sources of revenue, but this isn't so good for the club."

Regan stood. "I'm going down to the 13th Precinct. I'll give them your regards." As she walked out, Regan wondered when the next flight to London was leaving.

19

Over at the crime convention, Nora Regan Reilly was very pleased with the way things were going. The only disappointment was that Regan couldn't be there. So many people were asking for her.

"She was called on to a case," Nora kept saying.

"Since last night?"

"Yes, but she's still in town. She's going to try to drop by for one of the seminars. Or maybe even the cocktail party later this afternoon."

Nora made a quick inspection of the buffet the hotel had put out for lunch. It looked good. Steaming trays of pasta, chicken, and vegetables were ready for consumption. Nora had slipped out of the last seminar just before it ended to make sure everything was set.

It had been a most interesting seminar. An FBI agent had given a lecture and a slide show on con artists. How they manage to infiltrate people's lives, gain their confidence, and rip them off. Some of them were small-time crooks, whereas others could remove millions from their rightful owners.

"You'll find them everywhere," he had said. "They're like vultures that prey on everyone from lottery winners, to the elderly, to the lonely, to the ambitious, and to the vulnerable. Many people who get ripped off are then too embarrassed to report it. They think they should have been smarter. Big Hollywood celebrities get duped by investment advisers. People with less money get involved in pyramid schemes that collapse around them. It's bad out there, and these scam artists, when cornered, can be very dangerous. They lash out . . ."

The slide show displayed grainy photos of just a few of these people in action.

Yes, Regan would have loved this, Nora thought. What a shame.

"Mrs. Reilly?"

Nora turned away from the food table and smiled. "Yes?"

A rather imposing, breathless woman, with her hair swept up in a bun and a notebook in her hand, dropped her purse on the floor. "I'm Mary Ruffner, a reporter with the *New York World*. I was wondering if I could ask you a few questions about the conference."

"Of course." Nora led her to a table.

"Everything happens at once. My editor wants me to run over to Gramercy Park to the Settlers' Club. Some guy who just got sprung from jail is filming a movie there, and the rumor is that someone was murdered in the club last night." Mary laughed mirthlessly. "As long as he doesn't expect me to spend the night there. I write about arts and entertainment."

Nora's stomach took a dive as her smile faded.

"Anything wrong, Mrs. Reilly?"

"No," Nora said.

"Your daughter's here too, isn't she?"

"She's in town."

"I know that. Her picture was in our paper this morning."

Now it was Nora's turn to laugh mirthlessly.

"Is she at the convention?" Mary Ruffner continued.

"Actually, she's working," Nora said.

"On a case?"

"Well, yes, she's working in New York, but I'm not at liberty to say on what."

"I hope I get to interview her before the weekend's over," Mary said as she pulled the cap off her pen with her teeth.

Something tells me you will, Nora thought. For better or worse, something tells me you will.

20

Lydia sat propped up on one of her love seats, cordless phone in hand, calling all her lovelorn pups who had been present the night before. There had been nineteen of them. Not bad, she decided. She'd been having three parties a week since Valentine's Day, and as an introductory offer, her "clients" had only had to pay twenty-five dollars a shot if they'd bought a package of four.

She had to admit she felt like she was stealing from some of them. Like the man who wore sandals with his suit and seemed to end every sentence with the phrase "and stuff like that." Or the fortyish woman who hung on to her Snoopy purse all night, as though it were a security blanket. Actually, Lydia thought, it's too bad those two didn't hook up. There should be someone for everyone out there.

By the time she had finished making her calls, talking to some and leaving messages for others, ten had said they'd be glad to come by, a couple had told her they wanted their money back, and three more said they'd prefer to meet a new batch of people.

"Why would I want to come back tonight?" one guy had said. "Nobody there was my type. Isn't the club's big anniversary party going to have new people at it?"

"Yes," Lydia had answered optimistically.

"I'll see you then."

After he hung up, Lydia had added his name to her list of those who wouldn't be in attendance. She'd give the list to Regan later.

Lydia felt suddenly unsettled. What if it was someone in this group who had stolen the diamonds? She was in the business of welcoming strangers into her home. She'd invested her money in a business that could actually be dangerous. She never did background checks on people who came to her parties. How could she?

There were so many creeps out there. She'd met enough of them in her thirty-eight years of being single. She wanted her business to be a happy one. She wanted Meaningful Connections to bring love into people's lives in New York City. She wanted to boast the most marriages of any dating service.

Lydia looked at her watch. She wished Maldwin would get back soon. It would be at least another hour.

Her phone rang. She pressed the button and answered in a cheerful tone. "Meaningful Connections."

"Lydia, I want to come to your parties."

Lydia's face flushed. "Burkhard, no. I told you I don't want to see you anymore."

"You can't keep me away."

"Yes I can."

"I love you, Lydia."

"No you don't." Lydia pictured her recent boyfriend, who at first seemed so impressive. It didn't take long to realize that behind the one expensive suit he owned, there was nothing there. He took Lydia for granted, then when she dissed him, he hounded her. The guy had no job, no employment record—it was as if he appeared out of thin air.

"I'm going to join the club."

"Burkhard, please, just go away."

"I always get what I want," he said in a tone that, if it weren't so scary, would have been pathetic, like that of a spoiled child.

"You can't come to my parties."

"Then I'll see you at the anniversary party. And I want to get a picture taken with you, Lydia. I know the press will be there. I'm sure they'd be interested to know how you make fun of all your clients."

"I do not!" Lydia shouted, but the phone clicked in her ear.

"Why did I ever have to meet him?" Lydia screamed as she threw the phone across the room. She felt as if she were about to throw up. No one would want to sign up for a dating service if they thought the owner was unsympathetic. Or if they thought the matchmaker herself made terrible choices in her own dating life. It's like going to a dentist who has bad teeth.

What am I going to do? she thought frantically. What am I going to do?

21

When Regan met Detective Ronald Brier, she immediately liked him. He was in his late thirties, with brown hair, a stocky build, and a twinkle in his eye.

Regan sat across from him at his desk in the 13th Precinct. She'd walked over, glad for the chance to get some fresh air and clear her head.

"So you're a friend of Jack Reilly's?"

Regan smiled. "Yes."

"I remember the reports after your father was kidnapped." He shook his head. "How is he doing?"

"Never better," Regan assured him. "We were very lucky."

Ronald had the police reports in front of him. "You're staying at the Settlers' Club now?"

"For the weekend. My friend Thomas Pilsner is the president."

Ronald rolled his eyes. "That guy's very excitable."

"He cares a lot," Regan said.

"Yeah, yeah."

Regan leaned forward. "Tell me your impressions from last night."

"We got the call that the old guy was found in the tub. There was no forced entry. No bruising. No sign of foul play. Your friend Pilsner says that he saw the diamonds yesterday. Now, they could have been with the other guy, Ben Carney, who had the heart attack. As you know, his wallet was stolen."

"Yes." Regan paused, then continued slowly, "The red box that the diamonds were in was found in Thomas's office wastebasket this morning."

"No diamonds?"

"No diamonds."

"You don't think your friend was involved?"

"Absolutely not."

"Who knows? They were going to sell them, maybe Ben Carney took them out of the box after their lunch and stuck them in his wallet. Threw the box in the wastebasket in Pilsner's office on the way out. His office isn't far from the front door of the club."

"So whoever stole Ben's wallet could have made off with four-million-dollars' worth of gems."

"Not bad for a simple pickpocket. I have to tell you, though, we'll be keeping an eye on Pilsner. See if he disappears to the Islands in a few months."

"I don't think that's going to happen. I'm going to talk to people in the club this weekend. See what I can find out. I have a feeling that Nat's death is tied to the diamonds."

Brier just looked at her and waited.

Regan shrugged. "It's too much of a coincidence for me that the diamonds disappear and Nat dies the same night. To say nothing of the fact that the co-owner of the diamonds drops dead in the street."

"Ben Carney died of a heart attack. No question about it," Brier said flatly.

"By the way, where is Ben's body?"

"At the morgue. Apparently he has a niece in Chicago. They're trying to reach her."

"Could you let me know when you do? I'd like to talk to her."

"No problem."

"Tonight I'm going to a party across the hall from Nat's apartment. The woman who lives there is trying to get most of the people back who were there at her singles party last night. I might ask you to do some checks on them." She pulled the red box out of her purse. It was wrapped in a plastic bag. "Can you run this for prints?"

"I'd be happy to. We'll do anything to be of assistance." He paused. "Regan, there's no record of these diamonds. Pilsner is the only one who saw them. There's no appraisal slip. This could be much ado about nothing. If they do exist, they might be worth a heck of a lot less than four million dollars."

"I understand," Regan said. "But for these next few days I'll be the in-house detective at the Settlers' Club. I'll see what I can dig up." She stood and extended her hand to him.

"Jack Reilly's a great guy."

"I know," she said, smiling.

◆

22

Janey pulled a sizzling-hot apple pie out of the oven. Her little one-bedroom apartment a few blocks from the Settlers' Club always had delicious smells wafting from it. If it wasn't the baked goods she was making for dessert, it was one of her specialties such as lasagna or meat loaf or any one of the other comfort foods she enjoyed preparing for her clients.

She loved going into their apartments and filling their refrigerators and freezers with her plastic containers full of food. It excited her to think of them coming home after a hard day and zapping her loving efforts in the microwave. And now she was preparing some special desserts for the anniversary party at the club, including a huge tiered white cake they'd display on a big white table decorated with red ribbons.

Anything to cheer Thomas up.

Hey, I lost two clients yesterday, she thought. Nat and Ben had both loved her cooking. She had even dropped food off at Ben's apartment yesterday when he was out. Now it'll just go to waste, she thought.

It had been a busy week, and after she finished preparing the cakes and pies, she planned to go back to the club. Her phone rang just as she was placing the apple pie under the window to cool. It was Mrs. Buckland, a good but demanding client.

"Janey, I'm having three unexpected guests for dinner and I need food."

"But Mrs. Buckland . . ." Janey began.

"I know you can do it, Janey. Didn't I introduce you to all my friends?"

Janey held the phone in her hand, trying to figure out what to do. After a moment, she said, "Okay, Mrs. Buckland. What time do you need it?"

"In a couple of hours. Thank you."

Janey replaced the phone in its cradle. "I don't want to go food shopping now. And all that cooking. I don't even have time!" she wailed in a ladylike voice.

A thought came to her that she didn't even want to entertain. But like most crazy thoughts, if you give it a minute or two, it can take on a surprising sanity.

The food she had delivered to Ben's apartment yesterday had obviously not been eaten. Heck, she'd probably never get paid for it anyway, and she still had the keys.

It was a lovely roast chicken with stuffing, mashed potatoes, and her special gravy. She'd also prepared peas and carrots, baby corn, and a key lime pie. It was enough for two meals for Ben, four for people with less hearty appetites.

Well, why not? He had lived in a walk-up, so there was no doorman. She'd ring the bell. If someone was there, she'd say she was only stopping by to express her sympathy.

Quickly untying her apron, Janey grabbed her coat, purse, Ben's keys, and the bright-red thermal carrying case with her logo on the side, and ran out the door.

23

"Action!" Jacques Harlow cried to his assembled group of actors in the parlor of the Settlers' Club.

Daphne was sitting in the corner, out of the way, looking longingly at her fellow thespians who had actually been hired to act. Being a stand-in helped pay the bills, but all you really did was stand around while they set up the lights and the camera. Then when they're ready, they kick you out and the "first team" comes in.

It was dispiriting.

She stared at the sheep that had been in Nat and Wendy's apartment for so many years. Even though Wendy had been twenty years older, she and Daphne had become good friends. They'd sit and knit together or take walks around the park or sometimes Wendy would come down to Daphne's apartment for a glass of wine when Nat's poker-playing group got rowdy When Wendy became ill, Daphne promised to look after Nat, which she was more than willing to do. But he only wanted to spend time with his poker buddies. And those sheep!

"Don't talk to me like that!" the lead actress was yelling as she backed toward the fireplace. "It makes me really mad!" Her leg hit Dolly the sheep, and she lost her balance, landing in a heap on the floor.

Thomas, who'd been watching from the doorway, screamed.

"Get him out of here!" the director cried.

Thomas ran out into the hallway, down the front steps, and out the door. He thought he'd have a moment of peace, but cable-television producer Stanley Stock was standing right there, his camera aimed at all the movie trucks. Thomas had turned around to go back inside when he heard Regan's voice calling him.

Five minutes later, it somehow came to pass in the way that things sometimes do even though you can't really explain how it happened, that Thomas, Stanley, Regan, and Daphne, who had been given a break, were seated at a back table in the dining room, far away from the movie cameras.

"Don't worry, Thomas, I'm on your side," Stanley was saying as he buttered his bread. "I want to do a lovely piece on your hundredth anniversary here. I want to talk about how the club has in-house butlers, how it's a place to meet people thanks to an in-house dating service, how even Hollywood has come calling."

"Thank you, Stanley."

"Of course, one of your neighbors out there sees it differently."

"Who?"

"Archibald Enders and his wife think you're dragging the good name of Gramercy Park through the mud." Stanley took a big bite of the warm and crusty Italian bread. "They're waging a campaign to oust you."

"Miserable people!" Thomas growled.

"Thomas has been doing a great job," Daphne said with fervor. "No one who lives here wants this club to close. Since Thomas has come in he's worked very hard to improve things around here."

"Thank you, Daphne," Thomas said with a slight smile. "I know how hard this must be for you. You've lived here for a long time, and you were friendly with Nat."

"I knew his wife better. But Nat was a good man."

Regan felt a sudden restlessness. "Stanley, you were here last night at the party, right?"

"Indeed. And now I'm coming back tonight. Lydia's having the whole group back."

"So you were taping a lot of what went on last night?"

"Oh yes."

"Do you think I could see those tapes?"

"When?"

"This afternoon. Do you have them with you?"

"No. They're down at my studio."

"Can I see them after lunch?"

Stanley's brain suddenly fixed on the idea that there could be some excitement in the fact that his tapes might hold the key to a crime. "Of course."

If I can only find out who Buttercup is, Regan thought. . . .

24

It didn't take long for Jancy to find herself standing outside the old brownstone that Ben Carney had lived in for thirty years. After his divorce, Ben had wanted to live closer to the club. He'd been thrilled to find an apartment just a few blocks south of the club, within walking distance of his home away from home.

Janey took a deep breath and pushed the buzzer labeled CARNEY. She waited. The air felt raw, and she shivered underneath her beige wool coat. She looked up and down the street. There was no one around. Janey pulled out the keys and let herself into the vestibule where the mailboxes were located. She could see that the one marked CARNEY had mail in it.

So far, so good, she thought. She unlocked the

second door, stepped inside, shut the door behind her, and hurried up the staircase. Ben's apartment was on the second floor at the top of the stairs.

Janey stopped at Ben's door, unlocked it quickly, and pushed it open. It rumbled slightly. She ducked into the apartment, bolted the door behind her, and breathed a sigh of relief. I can't believe I'm doing this, she thought.

The whole place was eerily quiet. Even though the apartment was neat, it seemed to Janey to have a neglected, sad air, as though it knew the owner wasn't coming back. Just yesterday she had been here bringing food . . .

And now I'm coming to take it away! Janey pushed the thought from her mind and went down the hallway into the kitchen. It was big and old-fashioned, with a small butler's pantry/closet off to one side. Janey placed her thermal carrying case on the floor next to the refrigerator, opened the door, and proceeded to empty the refrigerator of her home-cooked meal. Her chicken, potatoes, vegetables, stuffing, and pie safely tucked in her case, she opened the freezer to see what else she might salvage. Janey laughed. A Tupperware container full of lasagna. She grabbed it and bent down to place it on top of the vegetables.

Suddenly she felt a presence. In an instant a

hand came from behind and sprayed her eyes with Mace.

"Aaaah!" Janey cried as she struggled with her attacker. But her eyes were burning, and she was thrown completely off balance. Within seconds she had been pushed into the tiny, dark closet, with the door slammed shut and locked behind her.

"Let me out!" she cried as she banged on the impossibly heavy door. But it was no use. She knew whoever threw her in here wasn't going to let her out. She was lucky they hadn't really hurt her.

She sank to the floor in the near darkness, just a sliver of light from the kitchen filtering in from the crack under the door. The reality of what had just happened started to hit her. Oh my God! she thought. This is humiliating! How can I ever live this down? If I'm ever rescued, Thomas will surely dump me! As her tears started to flow, she decided that if she did get out, Mrs. Buckland could cook for herself from now on.

25

Archibald Enders and his wife, Vernella, had long enjoyed living on Gramercy Park. Both in their seventies, they had traveled the world over but were always happy to come back to the town house where Archibald had grown up and give their staff a hard time. They weren't happy if there wasn't something to complain about.

The Settlers' Club virtually falling apart right across the street from them gave them a lot of fat to chew on. Archibald made sure he knew every disgraceful thing that was going on there.

As a boy walking docilely in the park with his nanny, as a lad on holiday from prep school, as a Harvard-educated young broker in the family firm, invited to teas and formal dinners at the Settlers' Club, Archibald could remember when the club had been worthy of its surroundings. But it had been in decline for the last quarter of a century. The rumblings of commercialism had become a stampede. Now its new president was turning the place into a tacky madhouse.

Home to a dating service! The setting for a third-rate film!

And all the hoopla last night, with the wailing of police sirens and the shrill of an ambulance. All the people out on the street stopping to gawk. Whispers of diamond theft and murder!

Not such good publicity for an old club that was trying to attract new members. The Settlers' Club will close its doors, he thought. No doubt about it. It will soon be occupied by someone more worthy of the surroundings.

And come to think of it, I have just the one.

He put through his second call to England that day.

"Thorn," he said into the phone. "I suggest you get over here on the last flight out tonight. We've got work to do this weekend."

26

Regan and Stanley cabbed it down to the converted gas station.

Now I've seen everything, Regan thought as Stanley escorted her inside.

"What do you think?" he asked with a big smile. "Other people convert warehouses into palatial apartments. I turned a gas station into a cozy home."

"You're a genius," Regan said.

"Thank you. Please sit down."

Regan sank into the couch, still amazed at her surroundings. She'd seen a lot of crazy abodes in her day, but this one took the cake.

"Would you like a cup of tea?" Stanley asked.

Fill 'er up, Regan wanted to say, but thanked him and accepted a cup of special herbal tea that

Stanley assured her cleared everyone's sinuses. I'm not really sure I want my sinuses cleared in this place, Regan thought. But the tea did taste good.

Stanley sat down and slipped one of the tapes from the party into the VCR hooked up to his big-screen television. The tape began with people milling around, chatting. The butlers were passing hors d'oeuvres.

"Pigs in blankets," Regan commented.

"Some people consider them low class. But they always go over well," Stanley said as he stared admiringly at the screen.

How did some of them end up in Nat's garbage can? Regan wondered . . . "What did you make of the crowd?" she asked Stanley.

"Generally nice people. Not everybody wanted to be on camera."

"How many didn't want their faces shown?" Regan asked.

"About half of them. As you can see, I still got the feeling of a big party. There's Lydia conferring with Maldwin and the other butlers in the kitchen . . ."

"There's a female butler," Regan observed.

"A hard worker," Stanley said vehemently. "A hard worker."

Now they were watching a man talking to a woman holding a Snoopy purse.

"That's some purse," Regan said.

Stanley sighed. "She hung onto it all night. As a matter of fact, she got very upset when the whole commotion started and we found out Nat Pemrod had died."

"Did she know him?"

"She said to me that she had met him at one of the other parties. He told her he liked her purse."

Could she be Buttercup? Regan wondered. Could one of these other women be Buttercup?

Regan didn't have time to watch every minute of the nearly four hours of tapes, but what she saw acquainted her with some of the people she'd be meeting at the party tonight. "What happened when the police showed up?" she asked Stanley.

Stanley fast-forwarded to the end of the tape, which showed a policeman standing outside Nat's apartment. Then it went blank.

"That's it?" Regan asked.

"I ran out of tape."

It figures, Regan thought.

"But they wouldn't let me inside anyway." Stanley pressed the OFF button on his set. "Was that helpful?"

"Yes," Regan said truthfully.

"You know, I take a lot of footage and then boil it down to the most interesting sound bites."

"I understand," Regan said, then lowered her

voice in a way that indicated she wanted to make Stanley a confidant. "Bring a lot of tape tonight, would you? I'll pay for it. Your camera can be another set of eyes for us. You never know what we'll pick up."

Stanley beamed. Maybe I'll get a network show out of this, he thought.

When Regan left, she hailed a cab uptown. It was four o'clock, and even though it felt cold and wintery, the days were getting longer and longer. Springtime was just around the corner.

Of course, April is the cruelest month, she thought. Although I think that for certain people March is a strong contender. Certainly for Nat and Ben.

I so want to help Thomas, she thought. But it seems as if he just makes things worse for himself. If someone from Lydia's party stole the diamonds or killed Nat, it's because Thomas allowed Lydia to invite strangers into the club.

But there was no sign of forced entry. Anyone who ended up in Nat's apartment, Nat must have known.

Regan took out her notebook. She jotted down a few thoughts. Talk to Clara again. Find out if there was anything she saw in the apartment that might indicate the presence of another woman.

Get a list from Thomas of everyone who lives in the club. Talk to the waiter who served Nat, Ben, and Thomas lunch. Find out who Nat's lawyer is. Where is the will? Finally, she wrote: Talk to the owner of the Snoopy purse.

For some reason, I think she's going to be pretty interesting, Regan mused as she leaned her head back and stared out the window.

27

When Maldwin and his posse returned to Lydia's apartment, he found her in the master bedroom with the covers over her head.

"Miss Lydia," Maldwin said to her. He knew that something was up. "May I bring you some tea?"

"I don't think tea will solve my problems," Lydia declared as she lowered her quilt.

Maldwin sat on the side of the bed. It was not something a butler of the old school would have done, but Maldwin believed that butlers of the twenty-first century should practice compassion for their employers. He felt he was Lydia's protector, confidant—in a way, her soul mate, even if she did occasionally drive him crazy. "What is it, Princess?" he asked.

"Burkhard called."

"That no good . . ."

"Why was I ever attracted to him in the first place?" Lydia implored.

Good question, Maldwin thought, but he tried to appear thoughtful. "At first Mr. Whittlesey gave an impression of class and breeding."

"Someone with class doesn't stick the lady with the check all the time . . ."

"I understand."

"Someone with class doesn't threaten to take things I said in private and twist them around."

"You mean about making fun of your clients?"

"Maldwin!"

"Sorry."

"He was only interested in my money. He thought he could manipulate me because he went to college and I didn't. But I've got street smarts."

"That you do, Miss Lydia."

"I'm afraid, Maldwin."

"There's no reason to be afraid," Maldwin said, even though he didn't believe it.

"I've invested so much of my money in this business. I want you and me to be a big success in New York City. We'll have our fingers on the pulse of dating and butlering for the third millennium. Burkhard could destroy that for me."

"We won't let him," Maldwin said firmly.

Lydia sat up. "How was your day?"

"A challenge. I'm afraid Vinnie and Albert do not have personalities suitable to a life of private service."

"I could have told you that."

Maldwin ignored her. "I thought they would be acceptable because my butler school is one for the changing times. It is impossible to think that you're going to find students who fit the mold of the classic English butler—the perfect Jeeves who seems like an aristocrat himself."

"Those two are far from it," Lydia agreed. "But as they say, good help is hard to find. I'm lucky I found you."

Maldwin winced. He hated to be thought of as "help." He ran the damn place as if it were his own. He cleared his throat. "As Meister Eckehart said, 'Everyone is born an aristocrat.' Unfortunately most people lose their charm in childhood."

"Who's Meister Eckehart?"

"A wise man." Maldwin stood. "We will prevail. Sunday night Stanley Stock's program will air, and I'm sure that on Monday the phone will be ringing off the hook. We'll get through this weekend and all its unpleasantries."

"And if Burkhard shows up for the party tomorrow night?"

"We'll handle it. I think we should focus on *our* party tonight."

Lydia pulled the covers back over her head. "I knew I should have taken that other apartment I looked at. I wouldn't be dealing with this right now!"

"Regrets are a waste of time," Maldwin said. "Now get dressed. We've got to make your gathering tonight the best one yet."

28

Back at their rented room, Georgette was sitting at the all-purpose table, examining the loot that she had procured from Ben's apartment.

It wasn't much.

She still couldn't believe that that woman, whoever she was, came in to take Ben's food. Talk about nerve. Well, at least she didn't see me. Who knows how long she'll be locked up there?

Georgette giggled. She looked up when she heard the key in the lock. Blaise came in looking as grumpy as he had when he left.

"What's all that?" he asked, pointing at the cuff links and foreign coins and silver brush-and-comb set.

"You'll be so proud of me," she said.

"Why?"

"Remember the spare key ring I stole from Nat?"

"Yes."

Georgette sat up straight, excited by what she had to report. "I had taken Nat's key off of it. But I got to thinking today. So I came home and looked at the other keys. In tiny letters, two were marked B.C."

Blaise's face remained impassive.

"Don't you get it? Ben Carney! Nat's best friend! The one who died last night! That's why Thomas Pilsner came running up to Nat's apartment in the first place."

"I know who you're talking about."

"I figured they had to be the keys to Ben's apartment, so I looked up his address and went over there. The keys worked!"

"Why did you do that?"

"Because he's dead. I thought maybe he had the diamonds in his apartment. You never know, ya know?"

"That was stupid."

"Why?"

"Because if you'd gotten caught we wouldn't have a chance to look for the diamonds in Pemrod's apartment. And they're more likely to be there if they're anywhere."

"No harm in trying," Georgette said, clearly

annoyed that Blaise didn't praise her ingenuity. And now I'll have to tell him the rest of it, she thought. Here goes nothing. "Someone walked in when I was in the bedroom going through Ben's stuff."

"What?" Blaise looked alarmed.

"Don't worry. She didn't see me. I sprayed her with Mace and locked her in the closet."

"Georgette! Are you out of your mind? All you got out of it was a few trinkets and someone who just might be able to identify you."

"I'm telling you, she didn't see me! And what if the diamonds had been in there? You'd be singing a different tune."

Blaise sat down on the kitchen chair opposite her and rubbed his eyes. "I just came home to get my tux. Lydia's having another party tonight."

"I'm going."

"You are?"

"Yes, she called and said she wanted to apologize for the confusion last night. So she's having the same group back tonight, no charge."

"I don't like the sound of that," Blaise said. "It's getting too hot around here. I think we should get out of town very soon."

"But what about the diamonds?"

Blaise thought for a moment. "After the party tonight, we'll both slip into Pemrod's. We'll search the place. If we don't find them, then I say we take off."

"What about your butler classes?"

"I can't stand them! I don't care about the proper way to iron the newspaper or draw a bath or polish the silver!"

Georgette picked up the tarnished silver brush she'd found on Ben's dresser and smiled at him. "You can practice on this."

"Very funny." He took her hands in his. "Georgette, something's up with Lydia. I can just tell. They're probably having us all back tonight so the police can question everyone."

"Maybe we shouldn't go."

"That would look bad. And I want to get a shot at going through Nat's apartment. Then we're out of here."

Georgette looked around. "I'll be glad to leave this dump."

"Me too."

"What if we get caught tonight?"

"We won't let anyone get in our way."

They laughed together.

29

Janey lay in the fetal position on the floor of the closet. Her eyes stung, and she was cold. She pictured her nice, warm coat draped across one of the kitchen chairs, just feet away. She still couldn't believe what had happened.

It almost felt as if her life were passing in front of her. All my hard work has come to this, she thought. A stupid mistake. Stupid, stupid, stupid. This definitely qualifies for an episode of "My most embarrassing moment."

Will someone find me? she wondered. Do I even want to be found? I could jump up and down, but I don't think anyone would hear me. This place is built like a fortress.

Her cell phone rang for the third time. It was in her purse, next to her coat on the chair. With my luck, it's Mrs. Buckland looking for her roast chicken. But in her heart she knew it was Thomas calling. He called her ten times a day. Sometimes if she was busy delivering meals, or stopping for a visit with one of her elderly clients, she didn't call him back right away. Like last night. So I wasn't there for him when he needed me.

Will he be there for me? He always has been. Will he even think to come looking for me here? Why would he? Who knows when they'll find the niece Ben always talked about? It could be days before they locate her and weeks before she comes to clean out the apartment.

And the anniversary party is tomorrow night! Janey didn't want to miss it. She thought of all the scrumptious desserts she'd made for it, the great big cake that would be a showstopper. All the help she was going to give Thomas recruiting members to the club. It was all too much to contemplate. Black depression was closing in on her as tears not caused by the Mace formed in her eyes.

After about five more minutes of wallowing in her misery, Janey made a decision. I've got to think positively, she thought. My life won't be over if I get out of here. How many celebrities have made big mistakes right in the public eye? All they did was apologize, some of them anyway, and then go on with their lives.

I know! she thought. Whoever sprayed that Mace in my eyes is a real criminal. They were scavenging through the apartment. Surely they must have stolen some of Ben's things.

If I get out of here, I'm going to do my best to help find them. Janey concentrated hard. Now let's see. It was definitely a woman. And I thought I felt long hair brush against my face when she shoved me in here. And her perfume! I'd recognize that smell anywhere.

The thoughts cheered Janey somewhat as she reached in front of her and pulled a box of what turned out to be Rice Krispies off the shelf. She stuck her hand in the box and helped herself to a handful. Snap, crackle, pop, she thought. That's exactly what I'm going to do when I get out of here and find out who did this to me.

She suddenly thought of her favorite movie, *The Sound of Music,* and began to sing softly, "'When the dog bites, when the bee stings . . .'"

30

Nat's answering machine light was flashing when Regan got back to the apartment. She pressed the PLAY button.

"Nat, this is Edward Gold. What happened to you and Ben? You never showed up today. We made a blowup of the check for the party tomorrow night. Give me a call."

Regan's eyes widened. She replayed the tape again. Who is Edward Gold? she wondered. And why didn't he leave a number? Was this a check for the diamonds?

She quickly called information. There were three Edward Golds in Manhattan. Regan called each of them. One was home. He didn't know what she was talking about. The other two calls she made were picked up by answering machines.

One called himself Eddie and the other Teddy. It was clear from their voices that neither one of them was the man Regan was looking for.

She was sitting at the counter in the kitchen. The Yellow Pages must be around here somewhere, she thought. In the second drawer she opened she found them. She pulled the heavy volume out, placed it on the counter, and opened it up to the Jewelers section. There were several pages of ads for jewelry buying, selling, repair, custom design, and appraisals. Estate jewelry bought and sold. Ear-piercing services. And then she found it. The ad for Edward Gold Jewelers, located on West Forty-seventh Street.

Regan picked up the phone and placed the call. In a minute she was speaking to Edward Gold. She told him who she was and the news about Nat and Ben.

"I can't believe it," he said. "They were in here just the other day. We appraised the diamonds and were going to give them the check today. Tomorrow night we were going to bring the diamonds to the Settlers' Club so everyone could take a look at them, and we had a blown-up replica of the check like they do for lottery winners. It was going to be such a blast."

"You actually saw the diamonds."

"I just told you, I appraised them! They're

beautiful. I even have someone who is interested in buying them. It's his fortieth wedding anniversary, and he was going to have them made into earrings for his wife."

"Some earrings," Regan said.

"I feel terrible."

"Did you know Nat well?" Regan asked.

"I knew that whole group who played cards together. What a bunch of characters. Can you imagine throwing a valuable diamond in a pot and leaving it there for all these years? Last one alive gets to keep all four. Those guys were funny. What a shame."

"How long did you know them?" Regan asked.

"About ten years. I met them at a jewelry show. They all retired a few years later. Sometimes they'd come up to the office for a chat."

Regan thought about "Buttercup." She wondered if by any chance Nat had confided in Edward.

"What is going to be done with the diamonds now?" Edward asked. "They were both so excited about donating the money to the Settlers' Club."

Regan hesitated. This guy sounded on the level. She looked at her watch. It was four-thirty. "I'm not sure," she said. "Do you think I could drop by your shop?"

"Now?"

"I know it's late on a Friday, but since the party is tomorrow night, and for the moment I'm handling Nat's affairs, I'd love to talk to you for a few minutes."

"Come on over. I've got a bottle of schnapps I was going to crack open with Nat and Ben. Maybe we should have a drink in their memory."

T hat last scene had to be the worst acting I have ever seen, Daphne thought. If this film is released and people know it was filmed at the Settlers' Club, no one will ever want to come here.

The crew was rearranging the lights and moving the camera so they could shoot from the other side of the room. Daphne was in the bar area, sitting by the actress she was standing in for. Her stage name was Pumpkin Waters. Cute when you're twenty, Daphne thought, pathetic when you're sixty. Clearly Pumpkin thought she was superior to Daphne.

"Work much lately?" Daphne asked.

Pumpkin gave her a withering look. "I'm always working."

"I know how hard it is when you get older in this business. Especially for women."

With each word, Daphne seemed to irritate Pumpkin more and more.

"It was interesting the way you incorporated those sheep into your dialogue. After you tripped over them, I mean."

"Could you please leave me alone?" Pumpkin asked. "I'm concentrating."

On what? Daphne wondered. She stood. "I'm going to go down the hall to Thomas's office. If they need me, tell them to give me a shout down there."

Pumpkin merely nodded her head.

Daphne found Thomas sitting at his desk, going over the plans for the anniversary party. As usual, he looked agitated.

"How's the movie going?" he asked.

"I don't think it's going to win any Academy Awards."

Thomas looked pained. "At least it will pay a few bills around here."

"Can you use any help for the party tomorrow night?" Daphne asked.

Thomas shook his head. "The kitchen has the menu all planned. Hors d'oeuvres. A lavish buffet. Desserts. Janey is making a special cake." He picked up the phone. "I'm getting a little worried. I haven't been able to reach her all afternoon."

"Maybe she's out delivering."

"She had no deliveries today. She was just cooking for the party."

"I'm sure she's fine. It's not even five o'clock. Where's Regan Reilly?"

Thomas put down the phone. "She's still not picking up," he said, distractedly, then he looked at Daphne and said, "Regan just left. She was on her way to see the jeweler who was going to buy the diamonds from Nat."

"So Nat and Ben had contacted someone about selling them. That's wonderful!"

"Not if we don't get them back! But at least it proves that they did exist. That I'm not crazy."

"You know, Thomas," Daphne began. "I never really approved of the idea of a dating service being run here in the club. All those strangers riding the elevators."

Thomas shrank in his chair. "Daphne, I allowed that for a number of reasons. For one, I thought that some of the decent people Lydia has in to her parties might end up joining the club. We need new members."

"I know, I know," Daphne said. "But that Lydia is so nouveau riche. And that butler of hers, Maldwin, thinks he's the only one around here with any class. I resent that. It's probably one of their guests who made off with Nat's diamonds."

"Daphne, stop it!" Thomas cried. "Regan is doing her best to try and figure all this out. She asked me to make a list of everyone who lives in the club so she can talk to you all."

"I didn't see a thing last night. You should have installed cameras in the elevator and the hallways like we talked about when you started working here."

"I was trying to save money."

Just then a production assistant appeared in the doorway. "Miss Doody, we need you now."

Daphne turned back to Thomas. "Let me know if I can be of any help."

Your kind of help is not what I need, Thomas thought but politely smiled. When Daphne left the room, he picked up the phone again. He was desperate to talk to Janey. But once again he got her voice mail. I know something's wrong, he thought. I just know it. If I haven't reached her by the time Regan gets back, I'm going to ask her to go over to Janey's apartment with me. With everything that had been going wrong lately, nothing horrible would come as a surprise.

32

The cocktail party was going strong in the main reception room of the Paisley Hotel. Law-enforcement professionals and the writers who wrote about their line of work were meeting and greeting each other with great merriment. The lectures and seminars had all gone well. People were already talking about the next crime convention and topics that would be of interest.

Luke had joined Nora for the party, and then they were heading out to dinner with friends.

"Have you talked to Regan?" he asked Nora.

"Not since this morning."

"I was talking with Austin today," Luke began as he accepted a glass of wine from the bartender. Austin was his right-hand man at the funeral parlors. "I told him about Regan's new assignment

over at the Settlers' Club. He said he knew someone who went to a singles party there on
Valentine's Day. It turns out that the girl who ran
it is the one we heard about last year who lived in
Hoboken. Remember the Connolly brothers
telling the story about the old woman who no one
knew had a lot of money and left it to her neighbor? The woman had been waked at their funeral
home and had planned a modest funeral for herself in advance. The Connollys had given her a
break on the price, then found out later she had a
couple million bucks in the bank!"

"I remember that!" Nora said. "I swear there's
more gossip in the funeral industry than any
other!"

"Well, this girl inherited all the money, and the
Connollys barely broke even. Now she's in a penthouse apartment at the Settlers' Club and is running a dating service. Then when the Connollys
had a charity drive, and they solicited a contribu-
tion from her, she stiffed them."

Nora raised her eyebrows. "Well, did whoever
went to her gathering have a good time?"

"Immediately after the party he got back
together with his wife."

"Nothing like a happy ending," Nora said
wryly. "Maybe you should let Regan know."

"I will," Luke said.

Next to Luke and Nora at the bar was someone very practiced in the art of eavesdropping. The reporter Nora had spoken to earlier in the day had come back, at Nora's invitation, to the cocktail party. So why didn't you tell me your daughter was at the Settlers' Club when I mentioned it earlier? Mary Ruffner wondered as she waited for her drink. Now I have to make it a point to get down there today.

She tapped Nora on the shoulder. "How *are* you?" she gushed. She turned to Luke. "And you must be Regan Reilly's father."

33

I figured with a name like Gold, I'd better be a jeweler." Edward Gold laughed as he poured two drinks from the schnapps bottle. They were in a well-lit office above his shop on West Forty-seventh Street.

"But I have a friend named Taylor who can't sew on a button," Regan countered, smiling at him as he handed her a glass.

"That's a good one. Come to think of it, I have a friend named Baker who'd need a compass to find the kitchen."

They clicked glasses. Regan didn't really feel like drinking the schnapps, but she figured she'd better show a spirit of camaraderie. It might entice Edward to talk. He looked to be in his mid-sixties, with a shock of pure-white hair, a little slash of a mustache, and big brown eyes that conveyed amusement. He was about five feet nine inches tall and had a thin frame. Regan got the feeling he was always in motion. He had a habit of pulling on the left shoulder of his sweater every few seconds.

"To Nat and Ben," Edward said seriously. "May they rest in peace."

I don't think they're going to rest in peace until the diamonds are found, Regan thought, but she took a tiny sip of the potent liquid, winced slightly, then cleared her throat. "I didn't want to tell you on the phone, Edward. But the diamonds are missing."

His eyes bulged and his face fell. "Missing?"

There goes his commission, Regan thought. "Missing," she repeated. She told him the whole story. "They might have been stolen with Ben's wallet. If that's the case, a pickpocket got very lucky. Or they might have been taken from Nat's apartment. I thought that if I talked to you, you might have some useful information for me. I just have a few questions . . ."

Edward poured some more schnapps for himself as he shook his head and pulled at his sweater. "Ask away."

"Did you see these guys often?"

"Once every couple of months the whole card

group would come up. We'd have a drink in the office and then go out to lunch. It was fun. They called themselves 'the Suits.'"

"I heard about that."

Edward nodded. "Nat, Ben, Abe, and Henry. Hearts, clubs, spades and *diamonds!* Friends for life. I tell ya, I wish I had a close-knit group like that. I have a lot of friends, mind you, but to have a group of four that spent fifty years together . . . They had a lot of history. They lived through children, grandchildren, divorces, wives' deaths, occasional bickering. But every week they played cards. After Abe and Henry died this past year, Nat and Ben did a lot of soul-searching. They felt really bad about losing their friends. Neither one of them needed the money from the diamonds, and neither one wanted to spend it alone. The one hundredth anniversary of the club seemed the perfect solution. They figured they'd have more fun donating the money to the Settlers' Club and telling them what to do with it." Edward looked truly distressed. "They were so excited about the party tomorrow night."

"Do you think they talked about the diamonds to other people?"

Edward shook his head. "They said it was their secret. But you know how secrets are."

"Indeed I do," Regan said.

"They used to call Ben 'Big Mouth Ben.'"

"They did?"

"He would sit at the bar at the Settlers' Club and yap away. There was nothing too trivial for him to talk about. Nat was the quiet type, although he liked to tell jokes. Anyway, he and his wife, Wendy, were very calm and placid. Maybe all those sheep rubbed off on them. You've seen the sheep?"

"Oh yes," Regan said.

"Crazy, huh? Some people get attached to their pets. They got attached to their stuffed animals."

"Everyone gets attached to something," Regan said. "Now, I understand all four guys belonged to the club."

"That's right. Nat was the only one who lived there. But it was like their fraternity. They broke bread many times together in the dining room. Drink your schnapps."

"It's good," Regan said as she took a small sip. "Did Nat talk about having a girlfriend?"

Edward's eyes widened. "A girlfriend?"

Regan was evasive. "If he was seeing someone, he might have told her about the diamonds."

"A girlfriend?" Edward waved his hand. "Nah! He was a little bit of a flirt with the ladies. The waitresses at lunch always loved him. But I don't think he was seeing anybody. If he was, he sure never told me."

"This might have been very recent."

"Oh, I get it!" Edward said. "A girlfriend wouldn't be too pleased if she heard he was giving away diamonds. After all, diamonds are a girl's best friend." He laughed but quickly became serious again. "That's not appropriate. Nat is dead, after all."

Regan thought that the schnapps was having a little bit of an effect on Edward. "Is there anything you can think of about Ben that might help me? Any of his habits? Anything that might not seem important but really is?"

"Hmmmm," Edward said. "You know we all went to his house once. It was his birthday, and we surprised him. He was in the bathroom when his cleaning lady let us in. His journal was out on the dining room table. Boy, was he embarrassed. The guys really razzed him about that."

"He kept a journal?" Regan said.

"At least up until then. That day he'd been writing a poem. It was pretty bad."

"The cleaning lady was there?" Regan asked.

"She came in on Mondays. Ben said he could spend the rest of the week messing up the place."

I want to get into his apartment, Regan

thought. If he was still writing in that journal up until he died . . .

"I'm going to put an alert out to other jewelers about these diamonds," Edward said. "They're very high quality and will be easy to recognize. Although I bet they'll be taken overseas to be sold."

"Thanks." Regan figured what the hell and drained her glass. When she stood up, her mouth was tingling from the peppermint taste of the schnapps.

"Let me know what happens." Edward wrote his home number on a business card. "I live out on the Island. I'll be home all weekend. I'll have to tell my wife we're not going to the party."

"Somehow I don't think the party's going to be much fun," Regan said.

Edward came around from behind his desk. "Regan, you know the only good thing about this whole thing? Nat and Ben would have been lost without each other. Neither one had to hear that the other one died. Can you imagine what it must have been like when they met up in heaven?"

Regan smiled. "It is a comforting thought."

"I bet there's some card game going on up there now. Maybe when I die they'll finally let me play."

"I'm sure they will," Regan said.

"Now don't forget, if you do find those diamonds, I'll give you the best deal. The check's already made up. Certified too."

"I won't forget," Regan said. I should be so lucky as to find them, she thought as she walked out the door.

34

When they weren't traveling, or getting ready for an evening out, Archibald and Vernella Enders always enjoyed a cocktail in their living room at 6:00 P.M. They sat in two armchairs by the bay window, which looked out on Gramercy Park. If it was summertime, they would criticize everyone who walked by. As the days grew shorter, they couldn't get as good a look at people, so they had to find other things to harp about. Now that it was March they were pleased that, thanks to the equinox, people were once again becoming identifiable in the twilight.

"I made a few phone calls today," Archibald confided to his bride of fifty-seven years.

Vernella sipped her drink. Long ago she'd taken on the demeanor of someone with a terminal case of excess stomach acid. Frown lines worthy of Mount Rushmore were permanently sculpted into her face. "And?"

"It looks like the Settlers' Club is in worse shape than we dared hope."

"How wonderful," Vernella replied in her almost guttural tone. "That club has gotten on my nerves ever since the sixties, when they let in those hippies who pranced around the park in their flower-power tee shirts. What ever happened to good breeding? Good taste? 'Pioneering people' my foot! The Settlers' Club has been on a crusade to disgrace Gramercy Park for the past thirty years."

"Don't worry your pretty little head, my darling," Archibald advised. "Down at the bank I was told that the anniversary party they're having is a sorry attempt to recruit new members. But it's a hopeless situation, and it won't be long before I can buy the building."

"Buy the building?"

"Yes. Cousin Thorn needs a home in New York for his butler school. It would be the perfect spot. Then we, along with dear cousin, will help bring about a return of class to New York City. Thanks to Thorn's school, good butlers will once again be available. Unfortunately that profession has suffered a sad decline. That needs to be changed."

"We need a butler ourselves."

"It's so hard to keep help. They always leave. But we will have first dibs on Thorn's graduates and, of course, hire the best one. As you know, Thorn will be arriving late tonight."

"The guest bedroom is prepared."

"Tomorrow night we will dine here with Thorn and toast not only the destruction of the Settlers' Club as their party fails miserably, but also the demise of Maldwin Feckles's butler school, which is a disgrace to every self-respecting butler."

Vernella giggled, something she rarely did. "I wish it stayed light longer," she said. "We could get our binoculars out."

"You are a devil," Archibald said as he grabbed her bony hand. "You are the devil I fell in love with."

"Oh, Archie," Vernella said coquettishly. "I'm not a devil. I've been saying my prayers."

"And just what have you been praying for?"

"Just that the party tomorrow night over there"—she pointed with disgust at the Settlers' Club—"is a complete and utter disaster."

Archibald clapped his hands. "This is going to be such fun."

35

When Clara got home from her day of scrubbing the Settlers' Club, she was so darn glad she couldn't believe it. I'm going to get out of this uniform and put on my robe, she thought as she unlocked the door to her apartment in Queens. It had been some day. Here I was trying to help, and Thomas goes crazy when I show him the red box. She shrugged as she took off her coat.

Maybe I'll take a bath, she thought, but then remembered Nat's fate. Probably not a good idea, she decided as she went into the bedroom, undressed, and put on the fleece-lined bathrobe her sister had given her for Christmas.

"That's better," she said aloud. She pulled open a drawer and grabbed a pair of her woolly socks. "Now I'll be all comfy and cozy."

In the kitchen, she heated up some chow mein and poured herself a glass of wine. She carried a tray into the living room, sat down in her favorite chair, put her feet up on the hassock, and turned on the television with the remote control.

"Thank God it's the weekend," she said to the weatherman who was reporting on possible snow showers for the next couple of days. "I don't care what the weather's going to be, because I'm just going to veg out."

She gobbled her chow mein and downed the glass of wine.

The phone rang. It was her sister Hilda who lived in the Bronx. They talked every night.

"What's doing?" Clara asked.

"Not much. What's doing with you?"

"A little excitement at the club today. One member was found dead in the tub last night."

"Oh my."

"And then some jewelry is missing, but I found the red box it had been in."

"Oh my. You'd better watch out."

"My favorite show is coming on."

"The one about those crimes nobody can figure out?"

Clara smiled. "That's the one. Talk to you tomorrow."

"Okeydoke."

Clara hung up and eagerly turned up the volume on the remote control. As usual, she watched the program with interest, getting herself another glass of wine during the commercial. By the end of the program, when they made their daily announcement about being sure to call in if you had a weird crime to report, Clara was ready to dive for the phone.

"1–800 . . ." she said aloud as she dialed. When she was put through, she announced, "My name is Clara, and I work as a maid at the Settlers' Club in Gramercy Park in New York City. Today I found a red box that *four*-million-dollars' worth of diamonds is missing from. And the man who owned the diamonds slipped in the tub and died last night."

"Hold on, Clara, we're going to put you on the air. Can you repeat that for us?"

"Sure!"

A moment later, Clara was saying, slowly and deliberately, "My name is Clara, and I work as a maid at the Settlers' Club . . ." as it was broadcast to thousands of homes in the New York area.

36

When Regan got back to the club, it was nearly six-thirty. Lydia's party was starting at eight, and there were still some things Regan wanted to get done beforehand. She found Thomas in his office, looking pale.

"What is it?" she asked.

"Janey's been out of touch since she left here this morning. It's totally unlike her."

"You've tried to call her?"

"Of course I have!"

Regan felt sorry for him. He had been worried before, but the expression on his face now showed total distress.

"She was going to come over this afternoon for tea. Something must have happened to her, Regan. She would have called if she couldn't make it."

"Do you have a key to her apartment?" Regan asked quietly.

"I do."

"Should we go over there now?"

"Yes," Thomas said simply. With great dignity he stood up and reached for his coat. "If she's all right, then I'll be able to handle anything, Regan. When you're worried about losing someone you love, all the other stuff seems trivial."

When they walked out of the club, they did not notice Mary Ruffner getting out of a cab.

"Regan, what did the jeweler say?" Thomas asked, almost absentmindedly.

"He said that he had appraised the jewels. That he had the check written out to present at the party . . ."

"Do you think Jancy's disappearance has anything to do with all this?"

"Thomas, don't think like that," Regan cautioned. "In a few minutes we'll be in her apartment."

I've got to move now, Mary Ruffner thought. "Regan Reilly!" she called as Regan and Thomas started down the street.

Regan turned. "Yes?"

Mary extended her hand. "My name is Mary Ruffner. I was just having a drink with your mother and father at that terrific crime convention she put together. I recognize you from your picture in the paper today."

"Oh yes," Regan said, quickly shaking her hand. "Mary, this is my friend Thomas Pilsner."

"Hello," Thomas said.

Regan could tell he was frantic to leave. So was she. "We're in kind of a rush . . ."

"I don't want to bother you. I'm actually a reporter for the *New York World,* and I wanted to do a story on the Settlers' Club for its one hundredth anniversary." She looked at Thomas. "Aren't you the president?"

"Yes," Thomas said in a guarded tone. "Can I call you later? Or tomorrow?"

"Later would be better," Mary said crisply. She handed him her card. "It's easiest to reach me on my cell phone. I'm very anxious to talk to you." She turned to Regan. "Will you be coming to any of the lectures at the conference?"

"I'm going to try," Regan said honestly.

"Good. Then I hope to be seeing you both very soon."

Regan and Thomas said their good-byes and hurried a couple of blocks south, toward Janey's apartment. She lived on the fourth floor of a walk-up. Outside the building, they buzzed 4A. There was no answer. Thomas took a deep breath, unlocked the door, and ran up the steps two at a time. Regan was right behind him.

At the door to Janey's apartment, Thomas said a silent prayer, unlocked the door, and pushed it open. The living room was straight ahead. To the right were the bedroom and the kitchen. There was no sign of Janey anywhere.

"I guess you could say I'm somewhat relieved, Regan," he said. "But where could she be?"

Regan looked around the small living room. The apartment was neat and orderly. The furnishings were simple but tasteful. Regan could see that some of the framed pictures were of Janey and Thomas. The dinette table was covered with files. Regan went over and took a glance.

"She kept meticulous records about what she cooked for her clients," Thomas said.

Regan picked up a piece of paper that had been left on the table. It was a list headed "Deliveries made Thursday, March 11th." A look of surprise came over Regan's face. "She cooked for Ben Carney?"

"He loved her chicken," Thomas said sadly. "He ate like a horse. She was just saying this morning that she was sorry he never got to eat the chicken she made for him yesterday."

Thomas followed Regan into the kitchen. An apple pie was on the windowsill. Dozens of chocolate chip cookies were lined up on paper towels.

Several cakes were out on the counter, waiting to be iced.

"She wouldn't have left this stuff out for hours without covering it," Thomas said. "If there was anything she hated, it was a stale cookie."

The answering machine was on the counter, tucked in the corner. The light was blinking.

"Do you want to check her messages?" Regan asked.

Thomas nodded. "We have nothing to hide from each other."

All of the messages except for one were from Thomas. "Janey, this is Mrs. Buckland. It's six o'clock. Where are you with the dinner? My guests are arriving in an hour! How can we have a dinner party with no dinner? Call me! I'm very upset!"

"Let's get her number," Regan said quickly.

Thomas went and got the file. Regan dialed the number and identified herself to an irate Mrs. Buckland.

"We don't know where she is," Regan said. "And we're very concerned."

"You're concerned? You know what it's like to invite people over and all you have is a bag of potato chips to put out?"

Regan tried to cover the irritation in her voice. "Mrs. Buckland, when did you speak to Janey?"

"At about one o'clock. I called her up and told

her it was an emergency. At first she hesitated about cooking for me for tonight, but then I reminded her of all the people I'd introduced her to. So she said she'd do it."

"What was she going to make for you?"

"Roast chicken. I must say she does a good job with it. The turkey she makes can be a little dry, but the roast chicken is fabulous. On the second day it tastes even better."

"Mrs. Buckland, I'm sure you hope, as we do, that Janey is fine. In the meantime, why don't you take your guests to a restaurant tonight?"

"You know how expensive that gets?"

"I'm sure you can find a place that's reasonable," Regan said.

"I suppose it would be nice not to have to clean up after dinner," Mrs. Buckland said, her voice softening. "I hope Janey's all right."

"Thank you," Regan said. "We'll let you know." She hung up the phone. "Janey was supposed to deliver a roast chicken to her this afternoon."

They looked at each other. They knew that they were both thinking the same thing.

"Not my Janey," he said. "She wouldn't have taken Ben's chicken."

"Mrs. Buckland said it tastes best on the second day."

"Oh God, why?" Thomas asked.

"Let's call over there."

Thomas got out the file labeled CARNEY, and Regan dialed the number. There was no answer.

"What if she went over there and . . . and I don't know what?" Thomas wailed.

"The police have the keys to Ben's apartment," Regan said.

"We have no choice but to call them," Thomas whispered. "No choice at all."

Five minutes later, they were out the door, with plans to meet one of the patrolmen from the 13th Precinct at Ben's apartment building. They had no way of knowing Mary Ruffner was right behind them.

37

Maldwin and the student butlers were prepared for the evening's festivities. They were all
formally dressed and ready to serve. The hors
d'oeuvres were waiting to be popped into the
oven. Cheese and crackers and crudités were out
on the tables. Champagne was chilling in the
refrigerator.

"The Princess of Love went hog-wild with this
party, huh, Maldwin?" Vinnie asked as he ran a
comb through his hair.

"Never comb your hair in the kitchen, please!"
Maldwin scolded.

"Now while we are waiting for our guests to
arrive, I'd like to go over a few things with you. No
sense wasting time. Let's sit in the living room."

Vinnie, Albert, Blaise, and Harriet took their

places on the love seats around the room. Maldwin stood at the window and looked over the group. It was not exactly an inspiring sight. He cleared his throat. "Now, what is a silent butler?"

"A butler with laryngitis," Vinnie answered.

"Vinnie!" Maldwin scolded.

"A silent butler," Harriet began, "is a small receptacle used to collect crumbs off the dinner table and ashes from the ash trays. It is found in every good home."

"Thank you, Harriet," Maldwin said.

Harriet beamed at him.

"You all need to study the sheets I hand out to you. I'm going to start giving pop quizzes. But on to other things. As you know, Stanley Stock, the television producer, will be here again tonight. I'm going to suggest to him that he ask each one of you about your dreams of being a first-rate butler. Who knows? Your future employers may be out there watching."

"How exciting!" Harriet cried. "Can I go first?"

I'm going to get sick, Blaise thought. And I don't want to be interviewed on-camera. Last night I did my best to stay out of sight.

Lydia's voice came over the intercom. "Maldwin, I need you for a moment."

Maldwin looked at his watch. "You may relax

until the party starts. Now remember, this is an important one!" He strode out of the room with purpose.

Albert turned to Vinnie. "What are you going to say?"

"Beats me."

◆

38

In front of Ben's brownstone, a patrol car was waiting with its lights flashing. When Regan and Thomas rounded the corner, the stark reality of the situation hit Thomas like a wet blanket. A small moan escaped from his lips.

Regan hurried over to the car and introduced herself. Squawks were emanating from the radio. There was no doubt the presence of the patrol car was attracting attention.

Officer Dowling, a friendly young cop, greeted Regan and Thomas and walked with them to the outside door. They buzzed, but there was no answer. Dowling unlocked the door, and the three of them hurried up the stairs to Ben's apartment.

As soon as Dowling pushed open the door and turned on the lights, they all gasped. The place had been ransacked. Drawers in the living room were pulled open, their contents thrown all over the floor.

"Oh my God!" Thomas cried.

"Looks like a B and E," Dowling said. He got on the radio and called it in.

Regan and Thomas walked down the hall in disbelief, turning on lights as they went. The bedroom and den were also torn apart. "The kitchen must be at the other end," Regan said, leading the way through the dining room to the kitchen's swinging door. She flicked on the light.

"Janey's coat!" Thomas cried. "And the carry bag for the food!" He ran over and stroked her coat lovingly. "Oh, Janey," he cried. "Janey!"

"In here!"

Thomas looked as if he'd seen a ghost. Or at least heard one. Regan felt pretty startled herself.

"Janey! Where are you?"

"In the closet!"

By now Officer Dowling was also in the kitchen. Thomas pulled on the closet door, but it was locked.

"We're going to have to get some equipment to break down the door. This is a heavy one," Dowling observed.

"Janey, we'll get you out. But what are you *doing* in there?" Thomas asked.

Janey started to cry. "It's a long story."

"Does it have something to do with roast chicken?"

"Yes," she answered feebly.

Thomas turned to Regan and mouthed the words, "Waste not, want not."

39

That's a wrap," Jacques Harlow cried as the last scene ended with the sheep being carried out of the room by Pumpkin and her leading man, Lothar. "On to our next location."

"Next location?" Daphne said with a puzzled look on her face. "I thought that this was it."

"No. We're going to my loft downtown. That's where we will shoot the climactic scene, when Pumpkin and Lothar decide they are going to move to Australia and buy a sheep farm."

"Brilliant idea!" Pumpkin called from the doorway.

"No, Pumpkin, you're brilliant. A brilliant actress. You're giving a multilayered, textured performance that is going to knock the critics' socks off," Jacques pronounced with a wave of his cigarette holder. "When you picked up the sheep and hugged it, I was blown away."

"It's your direction!" Pumpkin said liltingly as she ran toward Jacques for one of their post-acting hugs. "I was so in the moment thanks to your trust."

"Well, thanks to your being in the moment, I figured out the perfect way to end the story. Now let's load up the truck. And don't forget the sheep."

Daphne sat listening to the two biggest phonies she'd ever met in show business, and she was more and more annoyed with each word. But when she heard that they were going to take off with Nat and Wendy's sheep, she jumped up. "You can't take those sheep. They belonged to a couple, now deceased, who belonged to the club and wanted them to stay here in the front parlor."

"We'll bring them back," Jacques said.

"I still don't think it's right. The president of our club isn't here right now, so we can't ask him."

Jacques walked over to Daphne and took her hand in his and kissed it. "I'm sure we can give you a real part in this final scene. If you'd like . . ."

"Playing what?" Daphne asked tentatively.

"The beautiful and wealthy owner of the sheep farm, who has just moved to New York."

"Let's go," Daphne agreed quickly.

Jacques grabbed his walking stick from his ever present assistant, raised it in the air, and cried, "We're off!"

40

S tand back," the Emergency Services Unit officer called out to Janey. "I've got the gear to break down the door."

"What gear?" Janey yelled.

"A hatchet."

"A hatchet?" Janey cried.

"A hatchet," he confirmed. "It's a beauty."

"Be careful," she urged, then remembered to add, "please."

"I'll try. How much room you got in there?"

"Not much."

Thomas whimpered. He and Regan were standing at the other end of the kitchen. The apartment was full of detectives, patrolmen, and emergency services personnel.

"Well, here goes." The ESU officer lifted the

hatchet over his head and brought it back down against the door. The metal head struck the heavy wood with a snapping, crackling sound not unlike twigs burning in a fireplace.

There goes Ben's security deposit, Regan thought.

It took several minutes, but finally bits of the door had been hacked away. Another few minutes and Janey was stepping through the jagged opening and running into Thomas's waiting arms.

Murmurs of relief and "good job" rippled through the kitchen. One of the police officers stepped into the living room to pass along the good news to the cluster of folks out there and in the hallway, including a couple of neighbors and the building's superintendent.

Regan stood back as Janey and Thomas locked themselves in a passionate embrace. She certainly doesn't seem as meek as she did this morning, Regan thought. Well, it's the quiet ones who will get you every time.

"Miss," one of the detectives said to Janey, when she and Thomas finally unhinged from each other. "I'm going to need to talk to you."

"May I use the powder room first?"

"Of course."

While Janey disappeared down the hallway with her purse, Regan decided to take a quick look in the bedroom. She hadn't had a chance to look for Ben's journal once they realized Janey was locked in the closet.

The bedroom was a mess. Ben's nightstand had been emptied onto the floor. His closet had been picked apart. Photographs, books, papers, and clothes were strewn all over. Regan lifted up a few of the papers, a couple of pairs of pants, and then she spotted a spiral notebook sticking out from under the bed.

Regan picked it up and opened it. It was Ben's journal! The first page was marked January 1st of this year. She quickly flipped through the pages The last entry was dated Wednesday, March 10th. Two days ago. Unbelievable.

It was a fairly brief entry.

Well tomorrow is our big day to break the news to Thomas at the club. It's exciting. The big party is Saturday. I told Nat I wanted to invite a date. He told me he's breaking up with his girlfriend. He said it would embarrass him to bring her to the party because of their age difference. I told him fuhgedaboutit!

Regan turned back the pages. There were more brief entries that didn't reveal much.

And then the one marked February 28th was longer.

> Today Nat and I went bowling. We got to talking about Sadie Hawkins Day. I said it was too bad there was no February 29th this year. Maybe some nice lady would ask me out. He started to laugh, and I knew something was up. Finally he admits he's been seeing someone a little bit. The sly devil! He said he likes her, but there's only one problem. When you get close, her perfume is so strong. I told him to go buy her a new bottle. I said maybe I'll find someone and we can go to the club's anniversary party together. Then he said he felt guilty. I said, about what? Wendy? She'd want you to be happy. He just shook his head and said he didn't want to talk about it. So I let it go. I still say a double date would be fun.

Regan flipped through the remaining pages. No name of the girlfriend. No other references to her. Oh, Ben, why didn't you ask Nat her name?

Regan dropped the notebook on the bed in frustration and walked into the living room. Thomas was sitting with his arm protectively around Janey as she answered the detective's questions. "Her perfume was kind of strong," Janey noted.

Regan paused. Perfume? But then she heard a voice in the doorway and turned her head quickly. Mary Ruffner was scribbling notes as she talked to Officer Dowling. ". . . so she came here to pick up the food she had dropped off yesterday . . ."

I can just imagine tomorrow's headlines, Regan thought.

41

By the time Thorn got his act together, he realized he would not be able to make a Friday evening flight to New York City. Instead, he opted to go into London for dinner in one of his favorite restaurants, spend the night in a hotel, and head to the airport in the morning.

A much more civilized departure.

One of the problems with living so far out in the country was that things had to be planned in advance. But Thorn wouldn't trade his situation for the world. His butler school was on a magnificent estate—the perfect setting for such an establishment.

Hours before daylight, Thorn lay awake in his bed at the Andrews Hotel. He was restless, tossing and turning so much that the bedcovers were turning into a knotty mess. He had an early morning flight, and the news from Cousin Archibald that he wanted to buy the Settlers' Club was too delicious to be true. Thorn expected to destroy Maldwin's career, but then to set up his own butler school in the very building where Maldwin had failed was beyond his wildest dreams.

Suddenly, Thorn bolted up in the bed. He had a brilliant idea. He would contact his friend in New York in the morning. He turned on the light and grabbed the hotel notepad and pen sitting by the phone. He jotted down some ideas and dropped the pad back into the night table drawer.

Turning out the light, he sighed happily. Within minutes he was fast asleep.

42

Back at the club, the phone was ringing off the hook. Members who had heard or heard about Clara's television announcement were calling in and complaining. To the right of the front door was the all-purpose mail room, reception area, and general epicenter for the club's activities. Whoever was working there answered the phones, greeted the guests, and usually watched a little television. Will Callan, a longtime employee who had no interest in retirement, was on duty when Regan, Thomas, and Janey returned to the club from Ben's apartment.

"There's been a lot of excitement tonight, boss," Will observed as he handed Thomas a stack of messages.

"Tell me about it," Thomas replied.

"Clara really pulled a good one."

"What do you mean?"

"I couldn't believe my ears. I'm sitting here working and all of a sudden I hear Clara's voice. I turn and look at the TV—it's one of those true-crime shows, and Clara's telling all about what happened here last night. I said to myself, 'Oh boy.' Next thing you know, the phones light up."

Thomas took a deep breath and turned to Regan and Janey. "That thoughtless woman! I don't think I can take much more. I would love to see what my horoscope predicted for today."

Janey reached out her hand to gently pat his. "Part of it is my fault."

You're right about that, Regan thought. "Listen," she said, "I want to run upstairs to Lydia's party and get the lay of the land, as they say." She looked at her watch. "It's already nine o'clock, which means the party started an hour ago."

Thomas held up the messages. "I'm going to get on the phone to Clara and then whoever else I need to call back. Then Janey and I will have a quiet bite to eat in the dining room. Why don't you join us for a nightcap when you're finished at the party?"

"After being locked in that closet all day, I almost feel like going dancing," Janey said.

Thomas looked pained. "Tomorrow night we'll dance at the party." He then added, "As Rome burns."

Will had been sitting at his post, listening to the conversation. "At least that movie company packed up and headed out. Boy, were they annoying. They even took Nat's sheep with them. I tried to stop them, but Daphne said it was okay and they'll bring them back after they finish the movie."

"The sheep are gone!" Thomas cried. "I want them back here for the party tomorrow night. I'll have to have a word with Daphne."

Will nodded in agreement and slowly blinked his eyes a couple of times.

"Could you get her on the phone?" Thomas asked.

"She went with them," Will said.

"Please tell her to see me as soon as she gets back."

Will gave Thomas the thumbs-up sign.

"Okay, Thomas," Regan said. "I've got to run. I'll see you later."

Upstairs in Nat's apartment, Regan quickly took off the pants and sweater she had worn all day. For some reason she knew that they would not be quite dressy enough for Lydia's party. She freshened up in the guest bathroom, reapplied her makeup, then pulled a black skirt and black leather jacket out of her bag. In another two minutes she was ready.

"Here goes nothing," she said as she left Nat's apartment, double locked the door, and stepped across the hall.

One of the student butlers answered the door. He bowed slightly as Regan stepped inside.

Lydia came running over to greet her. She was dressed in a flowing, low-cut, pink silk dress. It seemed to match the room. When she gave Regan an air kiss, Regan got quite a whiff of her perfume.

Oh great, Regan thought. Now anyone who wears perfume is going to be on my list of suspects. "How are you?" she asked Lydia.

"You wouldn't believe how busy I've been today," Lydia said, then laughed as if it was the funniest thing in the world.

Regan smiled. "I've been kind of busy too."

"Well, come in. I want to introduce you around."

There were about fifteen people in the room, many of whom were on Stanley's video. To Regan's surprise, Lydia started tapping her glass with a spoon and calling for everyone's attention. When the chatter died down, she began, "Oh yes, hello again, everyone. I'm so glad you're here tonight. Last night's fun was cut short due to the death of my dear neighbor. But we have also learned that diamonds are missing from his apartment. So, everyone, we're here not only to get a chance to know each other, but also to help out my detective friend—" Lydia pointed as though she were announcing the winner of a beauty contest—"Regan Reilly!"

As all eyes turned to Regan, Lydia clapped.

So much for subtlety, Regan thought. "Thank you, Lydia. And thank you all for your attention. You know, I could really use your help. Sometimes we notice something, but it doesn't really register until we focus on it. That's why I'd like to ask each of you what you remember about last night. You might have seen something in the hallway or in the lobby downstairs when you came in. It could be anything. I know you all were enjoying yourselves in here for most of the night. But think about when you were coming in and out of the building. Thank you."

As soon as Regan stopped talking, people turned to each other and started murmuring.

"Let's have fun again," Lydia cried as she turned up the CD player.

A guy with a bad toupee hurried over to Regan, his drink spilling slightly down the sides of his glass.

"You must have seen something. Let's sit down right here," Regan said, indicating one of the love seats.

He sat down next to her and stared into her eyes. "You know, normally I only go for blondes, but I think that I could like you." He quickly took a sip of his drink.

This is worse than any nightmare, Regan thought. "Actually, I'm seeing someone right now."

"Is it serious?" he asked, his eyes growing wider.

"Serious enough," Regan said, then found herself saying, "besides, I live in California."

He reached over and touched her hand. "I go out there sometimes on business."

Regan shook her head slightly. "Sorry, I really am involved with someone. Now tell me what you saw last night."

"Nothing." He got up and headed straight for the food table.

Jack should see the competition, Regan thought as she spotted the woman with the Snoopy purse. Regan caught her eye, and the woman came over to her slowly.

"Please sit down," Regan said. "That's an interesting purse."

The woman was somewhere between forty and

death. Regan had the odd sensation that she even resembled Snoopy.

"It's a conversation piece," she said.

Regan leaned over and touched Snoopy's nose. She got a quick glimpse of a hidden zipper underneath it before the woman pulled it away.

"Please don't touch Snoopy," she said. "I don't want him to get your germs."

Oh boy, Regan thought.

"And I didn't see anything much last night. But I'm very sad that Nat died. He was a nice man."

"Did you know him?" Regan asked gently.

"He came to Lydia's Valentine's Day party. He sat with me for a little while and said he liked my purse. Then he told me he liked sheep. He said he had a couple of life-sized sheep that he'd show me. We talked about them a little bit. Then I went to the bathroom, and when I came out, he was gone." Her voice trembled as she spoke the last few words. "I guess he didn't like me."

"Maybe he was tired," Regan said.

"The party was kind of breaking up. I guess I took too long in the bathroom."

"Didn't you see him again at any of Lydia's other parties?"

"I caught the flu," she said and looked at Snoopy. "You did too, didn't you?" She turned back to Regan. "Last night was my first night back."

Some witness this one would be, Regan thought. She could just picture her on the stand consulting with Snoopy. "Were these people all at that party on Valentine's Day?"

Snoopy's mom looked around. "Pretty much."

"A nice group, huh?" Regan prodded.

"They're all right. But a couple of these women really pour on the perfume. How do they think they're going to get a guy if you can't breathe around them?"

"Who wears the strong perfume?" Regan asked.

She pointed to the door. "One of them's leaving right now."

43

Jack Reilly woke up and looked at his watch. They'd be landing in London in a couple of hours. Inside the passenger section of the plane, most of the lights were turned out. Around him people's heads were lolling in various positions as they dozed.

I wonder how Regan is, he thought. If it's not too late in New York when we land, I'll give her a call. For some reason, he didn't feel good about her staying in that apartment in the Settlers' Club. And I made light of it to her, he thought.

Sighing, he reached under the seat for his briefcase. He pulled out the materials about the case he'd be working on with Scotland Yard. A suspected murderer had been apprehended in London. The British inspectors had him in custody and had searched his flat. Inside they'd found subway maps and pictures of New York, along with various phone numbers. Jack's buddy was the detective superintendent at Scotland Yard.

"We need you to come over and take a look at this stuff. See if it means anything to you," Ian Welch had said on the phone.

Jack was glad to help Welch, but he wished the timing had been better. Oh well, he thought. I'll be back on Sunday.

But as much as he tried, he couldn't stop the nagging feeling that Regan shouldn't be staying in that apartment alone.

44

I'm sorry!" Clara cried into the phone. "I'll make it up to you."

"How?" Thomas snapped. "Haven't you ever heard that once a person's or an institution's reputation has been ruined, it's very hard to regain?"

"My aunt regained her reputation!" Clara said triumphantly.

"What are you talking about?"

Clara sat in her chair. "A long time ago, when she was working in somebody's house as a maid, some jewelry disappeared. The poor old lady who lost the jewelry insisted it must have been my Aunt Gladys who took it. So she got fired. Well, a few months later they found the jewelry in the house. Turns out the lady was a little dotty and kept forgetting where she hid things!"

"It's not the same," Thomas insisted.

"But it was terrible. Aunt Gladys lost a lot of weight in those months. It was only when she got her reputation back that she went back to eating like there was no tomorrow."

"Clara, I am not calling to hear about your Aunt Gladys. I am calling to request that you do not talk to anyone about anything that goes on at the club. Reporters might try to reach you. Please don't say another word. Now do you understand?"

"Yes, Thomas. I'm very sorry but I'll make it up to you."

"How?"

"I know you've got the party tomorrow. I'll come in and work for free!"

That'll make a big difference, Thomas thought wryly. But Clara meant well. "All right, Clara. I'm sure we can use your help in the morning."

"I'll be there bright and early."

The phone clicked in Thomas's ear. He turned to Janey. "Let's go eat."

"You'd better call the members back first."

Thomas winced and picked up the phone again. "Here goes nothing."

45

Georgette escaped into the bathroom when Regan started sticking her nose around the party. *I knew we were running into a streak of bad luck,* she thought. *This is not good.*

Looking at herself in the mirror, she sighed. She unzipped her purse and took out her brush. As she fussed with her hair, she reviewed her options. By the time she was reapplying her lipstick, Georgette had decided that she couldn't leave. *It would look too suspicious. But after tonight, that's it. Blaise and I will search for the diamonds in Nat's apartment, and if we don't find them, we'll cut our losses and get out of town tomorrow. Who needs this aggravation?*

When she came out of the bathroom, Blaise was standing there with a tray of drinks. "Keep cool," he whispered. "We're out of here soon."

Georgette smiled, took a glass of champagne, and walked back into the living room. I'm not going to miss these parties, she thought. Having to make excuses to a bunch of losers, explaining why you don't want to go to the movies. Give me a break. Uh oh. Here comes Regan Reilly, acting so fake friendly.

"Hello," Georgette said. "Any luck so far?"

Regan shrugged. "The woman I just spoke to said she wasn't even here last night."

"I was talking to her. She's a friend of Lydia's from New Jersey. She called Lydia today and told her she was coming into the city, so Lydia told her to stop over. By the way, my name is Georgette."

"Nice to meet you. Is there anything you can tell me about last night that might be helpful?"

Georgette tossed back her blond-streaked hair, shifted from foot to foot, and lowered her voice. "You know, Regan, the big mystery to me is why I come to these parties. The guy with the rug who was hitting on you asked me last night if I like to take walks on moonlit beaches." Georgette chuckled into her glass. "Or lounge on sheepskin rugs in front of the fireplace."

"Sheepskin rugs?" Regan asked.

"Can you believe that? My skin crawls just thinking about it."

"Thinking about the rugs, or him?" Regan asked.

"Him! I've got nothing against sheep."

Regan laughed. "So why *do* you come to these gatherings?"

Uh-oh again, Georgette thought. "I bought the package deal Lydia was offering. I figured I may as well use it up. And you never know, lightning might strike. Sometimes I think finding the right guy is like trying to find a needle in a haystack."

"What kind of guy are you looking for?"

"Someone who is kind and caring. Sense of humor. That's really important to me. There are so many problems in life, you have to laugh, right, Regan?"

"That you do," Regan agreed. "I love your perfume. What kind is it?"

Georgette laughed shyly. "It's called Lethal Injection. My old boyfriend gave it to me."

Regan smiled. "And what happened to him?"

Georgette waved her hand at Regan. "Another loser. He expected me to take care of him."

One of the butlers accidentally bumped into Georgette. "Excuse me," he said as he held out a tray of pigs in blankets.

"Thank you," Regan said as she took one and dipped it in the mustard. "These are good."

"At the end of the night there are never any of

these left," he replied, moving on when Georgette refused any.

"So you didn't see anything unusual last night?" Regan asked.

"No. It was the exact same deal as this. The guy with the camera was out here. I think he's spending tonight with the butlers in the kitchen."

He certainly taped enough of the party scene last night, Regan thought. For the next hour she talked to the other guests. When she mentioned to Snoopy's mom that one of the women with the heavy perfume hadn't even been there last night, she just shrugged. "I get confused sometimes."

Most of these women are heavy on the perfume—and makeup, Regan noted. After all, this party is a mating dance. People try to look their best.

"Are you having a good time?" Lydia asked as she pulled Regan aside.

"Lydia," Regan said in a low voice, "I'd like to get the names and addresses of everyone here. I'd also like to know who was here last night who didn't make it tonight. I'll run a quick check on them. No one has to know."

Lydia's eyes narrowed. "It had better not leak, Regan. This is my livelihood."

"It won't," Regan assured her. "Don't forget. This is also for the sake of the Settlers' Club. Now,

I also need the names and addresses of the butlers."

Lydia inhaled sharply. "Maldwin's not going to like that."

"If he and his students have nothing to hide, then it shouldn't be a problem. This is standard procedure. I'm going down to see Thomas now."

"I'll put together the list and slip it under your door tonight," Lydia promised.

"The sooner, the better," Regan said. "I want to call everyone as soon as possible."

At a candlelit table down in the stately dining room, Thomas and Janey were recuperating from their day of woe. They had each had a salad and a bowl of pasta and were now finishing the last of their bottle of wine. Before dinner, Thomas had made the dreaded calls to several of the members, assuring them that of course the party was still on and everything would be fine. He had also put a cold compress on Janey's face and persuaded her to lie down on the couch. When they emerged from his apartment, she was wearing a pair of his sunglasses. Her eyes were red and swollen from the Mace.

When Regan walked in, she found them at the corner table, underneath the portrait of the founder of the club. He must be rolling in his grave, Regan thought.

"Did you sniff out anything up there?" Thomas asked as he wiped his mouth with a napkin. On the way back from Ben's apartment they had discussed the perfume Janey had smelled as well as the reference to perfume in Ben's journal.

Regan smiled wryly. "There were a lot of women wearing perfume. And everyone claims to have seen nothing." She turned to the waiter who had approached her. "I'll have a glass of red wine, please."

"I'm sorry I couldn't go up there with you," Janey said. "I just didn't feel up to it, and I look a mess."

"Don't worry about it. Lydia wouldn't have been too happy anyway. She doesn't want it to seem as if we suspect any of her clients, and if you had walked into a singles party while you're still recovering from a Mace attack, it might have seemed a little odd."

"Or people might think I'm desperate."

"That too," Regan agreed.

"But I'm not desperate. I have Thomas." Janey reached for his hand as he beamed.

And you'd better hang onto him, baby, Regan thought. Because something tells me you're going to bring the Settlers' Club into the papers tomorrow. And it ain't going to be pretty. As the couple gazed into each other's eyes, Regan took a sip of the wine the waiter had just put in front of her. I may as well continue, she thought. "I got the names of the perfumes all the women were wearing. I'm going to go out tomorrow and buy each one of them. Then we can see if you recognize any of them as the one you smelled today." Regan paused. "Whoever ransacked Ben's apartment might have no connection with the woman Nat was seeing. It could just be a coincidence."

"The Fragrance Foundation would be thrilled to know how many people are spritzing themselves," Thomas remarked.

"You might say the whole situation stinks," Janey said before she drained her glass and started to giggle.

How many glasses of wine have you had? Regan wondered as she smiled at Janey. I guess I'd get a little giddy too after being locked in a cold, dark closet for a good part of the day, not knowing when I'd be rescued.

"Clara's coming in tomorrow," Thomas announced. "In an attempt to make amends for her disastrous phone call to the crime show."

"I want to talk to her," Regan said.

"Of course."

After several minutes of small talk, Regan

stood. "Time to call it a night. I'll see you in the morning."

"We have a lovely breakfast here in the dining room. Why don't you come down?"

"Sounds good," Regan said. As she walked out of the room, she looked at her watch. It was eleven-thirty. I've been here nearly fourteen hours, and I only have two days left to solve this crime.

Crimes, she thought. With each passing minute, she was becoming more and more certain that Nat had been murdered. That's why she had to talk to Clara. She felt sure that Clara, unknowingly, had information that would be helpful.

When she got off the elevator and walked down to Nat's door, she could still hear a small group of people inside Lydia's apartment. The diehards, she thought.

Within fifteen minutes she was in bed in the guest room, the alarm set for seven o'clock. I want to get up early and take a good look through this apartment, she thought. There's got to be something around here that gives me a clue. Regan turned out the light and put her head down on the pillow. Five minutes later, she was asleep.

47

"Action!" Jacques Harlow cried to Daphne.

They were in his sparsely furnished, high-ceilinged, drafty loft on a deserted street in lower Manhattan. Jacques had signaled one of his assistants to turn on a fog machine as Daphne sat on the floor, surrounded by darkness, and began to rhapsodize on the benefits and sorrows of selling her farm. Nat and Wendy's sheep stood at attention on either side of her.

"I look out over the moors," Daphne almost whispered, "and my heart starts to sing . . ."

"Wait!" the cameraman shouted.

"Wait! What do you mean wait?" Jacques demanded. "The director is the boss! The director calls 'action' and the director calls 'cut.' How could you forget such a thing?"

"You're going to waste a lot of film. I'm getting a bad reflection off the sheep's eyes."

"So turn the sheep sideways and pull their bangs down," Jacques screamed impatiently.

Two weary production assistants hurried over. When they turned Dolly to face Daphne, one of her eyes fell out and rolled away into the darkness. As they frantically scrambled to feel around for it on the floor, Jacques screamed again. "Don't worry about it! I don't care about the sheep's eyes. I only care what's going on in my actor's eyes. Now turn the other sheep and let's go!"

Bah-Bah in place on one side, Dolly on the other, Daphne was ready to start over. The two sheep now looked as though they were dying to hear what she had to say.

"Action!" Jacques cried again.

For the next six minutes, Daphne emoted over her character's sheep farm like nobody's business. At the end, sobbing, she lowered her head to the ground as Scarlett O'Hara had done so famously in *Gone with the Wind*.

"Cut!" Jacques cried, his voice trembling. He wiped a tear from his eye and ran over to embrace Daphne. "I was so moved," he whispered in her ear as the crew broke into applause. "You're a magnificent actress. I want you to star in my next film."

Daphne was speechless. She hadn't felt this good in years. Both her personal and professional lives had been less than satisfactory. But all of a sudden, it seemed as if a whole new wonderful world was opening up to her. It sure beat stand-in work. "Oh, Jacques," she finally mouthed as she laid her head against his shoulder.

Pumpkin sat seething in the corner. She stood up. "Are we ready to shoot my final scene?"

"No!" Jacques sneered. "Daphne is going to do her monologue again for me. Her well is overflowing, and I want to capture more of it."

"Yeah, well I'm going outside for a cigarette," Pumpkin announced and turned on her heel.

Jacques gave Daphne a mischievous glance. "Would you like Pumpkin to be your stand-in?"

Daphne laughed as Jacques returned to his director's chair. She petted Dolly and Bah-Bah. "Can you imagine how surprised your mommy and daddy would be to see that you've turned into movie stars?"

48

When a thud sounded from Nat's living room, Regan awoke with a start. Her heart began beating rapidly. What was that? she wondered as she sat up and listened. Everything was still. The illuminated clock next to the bed read 2:11.

Regan slipped out of bed, grabbed her robe, slowly walked to the closed door, and cocked her head. She could hear the floorboards creaking. Oh my God, she thought. There's someone out there! Then the sound of muffled whispers made her realize that there was more than one person.

Regan's heart was pounding in her chest. Two people at least, and I don't have anything to protect myself with, she thought. And last night someone was murdered in this apartment. I can't go out there. Who knows what I'll find? She reached over to lock the bedroom door. But her fingers met with a smooth surface. There was no lock. Oh my God. I've got to get help. I've got to get help or I could end up like Nat.

She crept back to the bed, where she had her cell phone plugged in to the wall. Grabbing it with shaky hands, she dialed 911. "I'm at the Settlers' Club in Gramercy Park," she whispered. "There are intruders in the apartment. There was a burglary here last night."

"What is the address?" the operator asked matter-of-factly, as if she were taking an order for the local deli.

"It's on the park in Gramercy Park. Twenty-first Street."

"You don't have the exact address?"

"No. There may have been a murder here last night . . ." As Regan said the last five words, the bedroom door opened. There was a gasp, the door slammed, and Regan heard feet running down the hall.

"Please—the Settlers' Club—look it up," Regan pleaded. She dropped the phone and ran out into the hall. She heard the back door shut and raced toward the kitchen. By now her heart was in her mouth. If I can only get a glimpse of them, she thought as she ran through the darkness. In the kitchen, she flicked on the light, then yanked open the door. There was no sign of anyone, but she could hear footsteps descending the back stairway.

Running back into the kitchen and down the hallway, Regan picked up the house phone. A sleepy-sounding voice answered.

"Hello."

"This is Regan Reilly. I'm staying in Nat Pemrod's apartment. It was just broken into, but the intruders got scared off. They're running down the steps by the service elevator."

"Oh my goodness."

"Well, do something!" Regan cried.

"They must have gone out the back door."

"The back door?" Regan said in disgust.

"It's only used for emergencies."

Regan shook her head. "I guess this qualifies. The police should be here in a few minutes."

"I'll send them up, ma'am."

"Thank you." Regan hung up the phone and went around turning on lights. The living room had been ransacked. *I must have been sleeping the sleep of the dead,* she thought.

Books and pictures were all over the floor, and Nat's desk was torn apart. *I guess my room was next.* She shuddered. *What if I hadn't woken up until it was too late? If I'd have gotten away with* only a Mace attack like Janey, I would have been lucky.

I'd better let Thomas know. She went back to the house phone and called downstairs.

"Could you please call Thomas for me?" Regan asked.

"I already did. I was just about to ring you. The police are on their way up."

Thomas was getting off the elevator as Regan opened the door. He had on a crisp linen robe and leather slippers that certainly suggested gracious living. The police were right behind him, their radios squawking.

"Regan!" Thomas cried as he entered Nat's apartment, and for the second time in less than six hours, hugged someone involved in a crime scene.

"It could have been a lot worse," Regan assured him. "But I don't think they expected to find me in the guest room."

The two cops introduced themselves to Regan. "We were here last night," Officer Angelo said. He turned to Thomas. "How're you feeling?"

"Better, thank you," Thomas said as he and Regan followed them into the living room. "I appreciate your asking."

"They ran out the back door." Regan explained to the officers what had happened.

"No sign of forced entry?" Officer Angelo asked.

"None that I see," Regan answered.

"Just like last night."

"What happened?" Lydia cried, rushing across the hall with Maldwin right behind. They were both clad in their pj's and robes. Lydia's getup, of course, was worthy of a Las Vegas lounge act.

"Miss Lydia woke me when she heard noises in the hallway," Maldwin volunteered.

"Hellooooo." It was now Daphne's turn to make an entrance. "I just got back from my movie shoot and heard at the front desk that there was some excitement up here." She looked at the mess all over the living room. "When will it end?"

And she doesn't even know what happened at Ben's, Regan thought.

Since Daphne's question was rhetorical, no one answered. But Maldwin felt the need to say something.

"Perhaps I should prepare some tea for all of us."

"Not in here," one of the cops advised. "This is a crime scene."

"I had no intention of preparing it here, sir," Maldwin replied stiffly. "My kitchen and special teapots are across the hall."

"That's a wonderful idea," Lydia said. "Do you need any help?"

"Not at all," Maldwin said. "Whenever you're ready, come over."

The sight of him, bowing in his robe before he exited, almost made Regan laugh.

"Did you bring the sheep back?" Thomas brusquely asked Daphne.

"You'll never guess . . ." Daphne began.

"I guess that means no."

"My acting career has just received a renewed blast."

"Is Bah-Bah your new agent?" Thomas inquired.

"I resent that. But the sheep are starring in the movie too. We have more scenes to film tomorrow, so the sheep are spending the night at the director's apartment."

"I want them back for the party," Thomas warned.

"They'll be back."

"Promise?"

"Promise."

"Why don't you all go across the hall?" Regan suggested. "I'll be there soon. I want to talk to these officers for a few minutes."

"I could use a cup of tea," Daphne said.

After the group exited, Officer Angelo turned

to Regan. "Whoever did this is pretty determined. I don't think you should stay in here tonight."

"I don't want to."

"What will you do?"

"I'm sure one of them has a room I can crash in," Regan said as she pointed across the hall.

Angelo smiled at her. "Lucky you."

49

W e're never going to be rich," Georgette sobbed as she lay in Blaise's arms in their lumpy bed.

"It's Regan Reilly's fault," he said. "Who would have thought she'd have camped out there?"

"She never mentioned it when we were talking."

"Well . . . by the way, don't give out so much information. You were getting a little too chatty."

"She liked the perfume you gave me."

"Don't wear it again."

Georgette lifted her head and looked Blaise in the eye. "Why not?"

"Why do you think?"

"I don't know."

"Have you ever heard of hound dogs at a crime scene?"

"Yeah."

"They pick up a scent. Think of Regan Reilly as a hound dog."

Georgette put her head back down. "I won't use it again until we shove off from here. I wish we could leave now."

"Well, we can't. When I heard Reilly talking to the 911 operator about a murder, I realized we've got to stay put. If we disappear now, it'd be too suspicious. They'd really come looking for us. And I don't want to get nailed for something I didn't do."

"And I don't want to go back there tonight for the anniversary party," Georgette said. "We'll never get the diamonds. What's the point?"

"The point is that it ain't over till it's over. I've got a couple weeks of the butler school left, and then we're out of here. In the meantime, you sit and think about your boyfriend Nat. Think about where those glass stones might have come from and what he would have done with the diamonds."

"He loved to play practical jokes."

"It's really funny hiding diamonds worth millions."

Georgette stared up at the ceiling. "Whoever came into the apartment that night and murdered him might know what he did with them."

Blaise stroked her hair. "But who would that be?"

"I don't know." Georgette was suddenly irritated. "You don't think he was cheating on me, do you?"

50

When Jack arrived in London, it was just after 7:00 A.M. Which means it's just after two in New York, he thought. I hope Regan's asleep. He hadn't checked any bags, so he zipped through immigration and out to the taxi stand, where a driver was waiting for him.

Forty-five minutes later he was at the front desk of his hotel near Scotland Yard.

"You're lucky," the clerk said to him. "Your room is ready. The gentleman who used it last night checked out early this morning. The maid's already been in there and tidied up."

"Great," Jack said. He knew they didn't have to have the room ready until three o'clock, but he was dying for a shower and wanted to get over to Scotland Yard. He was restless but couldn't quite put his finger on the reason why. With any luck I can get everything done today and catch a flight back tonight, he thought hopefully.

He refused the offer of a bellman, since he just had a hanging bag, and took the key to his room on the fifth floor. When he reached the room, the maid's cart was parked right outside the open door.

"Hello," he said as he walked in.

"Hello, love." The fiftyish maid popped her head out of the bathroom. She was a cheerful sort.

"I'm sorry. They told me the room was ready."

"Right. They're always getting confused, aren't they? I'll be out of here in two shakes."

"Thanks. I have to shower and then get to work."

"So you're working on Saturday too?"

Jack smiled as he walked over to the bed and put down his bag. "Yes."

"It's a living," she said. "All right. I've finished up. Have a good one."

"You too," Jack said, then noticed money and a note on top of the dresser. "Wait," he called to her as she started out the door. "I think this money must be yours."

"Thanks, love," she said as she hurried over to the dresser. When she realized how little was there, she said, "Hardly worth the shoe leather to come and fetch it," but nonetheless shoved it into her pocket and picked up the note. "Thanks for such great service. It was like having my own butler." She looked at Jack and rolled her eyes. "Maybe I should become a butler."

Jack smiled. "I know of a butler school in New York City that just started."

The maid waved her hand at him. "We've got more than enough butler schools over here. Too many in fact. A lot of competition. But it doesn't matter to me. I'd never last in one of those places. Too formal for me." She headed back out the door. "Cheerio, love."

"Cheerio," Jack said as he unzipped his bag and hurried into the bathroom with his shaving kit.

51

Tea, Miss Regan?" Maldwin asked as he ushered her into Lydia's living room, where Daphne, Lydia, and Thomas were enjoying their second cup. It was now three-thirty in the morning.

"Thank you, Maldwin," she said as she sat down on a love seat next to Daphne.

"Well, what's going on over there now?" Daphne asked.

"The police are finished. They dusted for fingerprints and secured the apartment. They're locking the front door with a special padlock. Thomas, we've got to get the old locks changed first thing in the morning."

"Of course, Regan. Do you want to stay in my apartment tonight?"

"Oh I'd offer, but my apartment is a mess,"

Daphne jumped in. "Getting ready to do the movie was so hectic. There's stuff thrown all over . . ."

"You must stay here!" Lydia insisted. "There's a maid's room off the kitchen with a pull-out Castro convertible couch. It's safe, secure, and all yours."

"Maybe I'll take you up on that," Regan said. She'd slept on many a Bernadette Castro special in her day.

"The room is rather small, so I didn't want Maldwin to have to live in it," Lydia explained. "But it's perfect for your purposes."

Thomas had filled the others in on the break-in at Ben's. Of course, he had sugar-coated Janey's little drop-by. "She hates to see things go to waste," he had explained.

"Regan, with all that's been happening, maybe we should have more security around here," Daphne suggested.

"We can't have armed guards walking the hall-ways," Lydia answered. "This is supposed to be a place of refinement."

"You can't be refined when you're dead," Daphne shot back.

"We can't afford it, Daphne," Thomas cried. "Unless a miracle happens and we get those dia-monds, or if the cast of *Ben-Hur* decides to join the

Settlers' Club, I'm afraid we're in deep, deep trouble. We just may have to close down."

"My dating service!" Lydia moaned.

"My butler school!" Maldwin choked.

"What about me?" Thomas asked. "This is more than a job to me. It was my dream to bring this club back to life. Make it a vibrant place for gracious living and art appreciation. I even imagined we'd have a five-year waiting list for people to get in!"

"Five years is what it would take for me to find another decent apartment in New York City," Daphne commented, her voice rising. "I like it here and I want to stay. The Settlers' Club has been my whole life for the past twenty years . . ."

"Listen, everybody," Regan interrupted. "There's no sense in arguing. We all want the same thing. I suggest that we join forces and go all out to try and make it a fabulous party tomorrow night. It's the club's one hundredth anniversary. Stanley's coming with his television camera, right?"

Lydia nodded. "He'll be so mad he missed all this excitement."

"Well, we don't want this in his piece," Thomas pointed out. "We only want the good stuff about the club."

"I'll ask my parents to come," Regan said. "My

mother's running a crime convention, and maybe she can get some of her author friends to drop by."

Thomas bit on his handkerchief. "Good idea, Regan."

"We have to put on a good show. In the meantime, I'll be working with the police. Whoever broke into Nat's apartment tonight has to be stopped. They may be very dangerous. So keep your doors locked."

"What a day." Daphne sighed. "Although for me, it wasn't all bad."

Thomas stood. "Don't forget. We want those sheep back for the party. Maybe they'll be our good-luck charms."

52

When Clara's alarm went off, she groaned. It's my own damn fault, she thought, that I have to get up early on a Saturday. I got carried away when I called in to that show, and I certainly got more than carried away when I volunteered to work for free. She turned off the alarm and just lay there for a few minutes. I sure wish I had one of Maldwin's butler students here to bring me a cup of coffee. That would make getting out of bed so much easier.

Well, I don't think I'm going to have a butler in this lifetime, Clara reflected as she dragged herself out from under the warm comforter. The best I have to hope for is being reincarnated as a Rockefeller. She went into the kitchen and turned on the coffeemaker, then headed for the shower.

The warm spray felt good on her back and arms that spent so many hours scrubbing other people's dirt.

Wrapped in her robe, she hurried back into the kitchen and poured that first cup of coffee she always drank while getting dressed. I'm dillydallying too much, she realized. I won't have time for a second cup today. I said I'd get there early.

Twenty minutes later, she left the apartment in a pair of stretch pants, an oversized sweater, and her big winter coat. She always changed into her maid's uniform at the club.

March 13th and it feels like spring is months away, she thought as she pulled on her gloves. It was another gray, chilly, lifeless day. As usual, she walked the six blocks to the subway station. The streets were empty because it was early on a Saturday. When she got to the station, she walked to the newsstand and gasped when she saw the blaring headlines of the *New York World:*

CRIME SPREE AFFECTS SETTLERS' CLUB
CLUB PRESIDENT'S GIRLFRIEND STEALS FOOD
FROM DEAD MEMBER

Clara pulled a paper from the top of the pile and started devouring the story.

"Lady, you want to pay for that?" the vendor asked her.

Clara grabbed a couple of quarters from her purse without taking her eyes off the page and dropped them on the counter. One of them bounced into the candy section, but Clara didn't even notice.

"Thanks a lot, lady."

"Oh, you're welcome," Clara mouthed as she walked away, shaking her head. *And they were worried about me calling the crime show. I have half a mind to go home and go back to bed.*

The subway that would take her to Gramercy Park was heading down the track. *What the heck, I'll be a sport and help poor Thomas,* she thought as the train stopped. She spent the entire trip into Manhattan shaking her head and going over every word of the article.

53

The maid's room was cozy all right. So cozy that when you opened the door, it slammed into the couch. But Regan didn't mind. By the time she retired for the second time that night it was four o'clock. Talk about musical beds, she thought as she pulled the covers over her and turned to face the wall.

Sleep didn't come as quickly as it had in Nat's guest room. And when it did, it was in fits and starts, accompanied by strange dreams that she could barely remember. It was only when light started coming through the window that she finally fell into a deeper sleep.

At ten after nine her cell phone rang. Regan opened her eyes and looked around, momentarily confused. Then, like a boomerang, the memories of the last twenty-four hours all came back to her. She reached for her phone on the nightstand next to the bed. The Caller ID showed her parents' number.

"Hi," she answered and realized she sounded pretty tired.

"Regan, are you all right?" Nora asked with concern.

"Yes. I'm just not fully awake."

"So you haven't seen the paper yet?"

"No, but now it's safe to say I'm wide awake. How bad is it?"

"Pretty bad."

"What page?"

"The front page." Nora read the headline.

"That'll make Thomas's day."

"The article makes it sound like all hell is breaking loose at the Settlers' Club."

"It is, Mom." Regan admitted, knowing she had to tell her mother what happened.

"What do you mean?"

"Last night, when I was sleeping, Nat Pemrod's apartment was broken into."

"Regan, oh my God! Are you all right?"

"Yes." Regan gave Nora a full explanation of the nocturnal excitement, concluding, "I slept in the maid's room in the apartment across the hall."

"The apartment with all those butlers and singles parties?"

"How'd you guess?"

"It's in the article." Nora relayed the conversation to Luke, who was next to her.

Regan sighed and rubbed her eyes. "I can't wait to read it. I'm surprised Thomas hasn't come running up here already this morning. Wait till that reporter gets her hands on the crime blotter with the latest incident. By the way, she made it seem like you were her buddy."

"She's covering the crime convention, but I think she found what's going on at the Settlers' Club more interesting. Listen to this:

"'While Nora Regan Reilly is uptown running a crime convention for writers of fiction, daughter Regan is investigating the real thing in toney Gramercy Park. And boy does she have her hands full.'"

Regan sat up. "That I do."

Nora continued. "'When the senior Reilly was asked about her daughter's whereabouts, she said Regan was working on a case in New York but refused to get specific . . .'"

"So much for classified information."

"Why must they refer to me as the 'senior' Reilly? I hate that."

"At least she didn't call me junior."

"Yes she did."

"Why don't I just get the paper and read it myself? Listen, Mom, do you think you could round up some of your cronies from the convention and drop by the party tonight? We're trying to make this gathering as interesting as possible. Divert the attention from what's gone on, although with everything in the news now, that seems unlikely. We've got a lot of damage control to take care of."

"What time does the party start?"

"Seven."

"That'd work. Our cocktail hour is from five-thirty to six-thirty, and then people are on their own until the final sessions and brunch tomorrow. I'll see who wants to come down. Before you hang up, your father wants to talk to you."

"Okay."

"Hi, honey," Luke said. "Be careful, would you?"

Luke and Regan both chuckled. It was a family joke. Once after she had slipped and fallen in the snow, Nora had leaned over Regan, who was sprawled on the sidewalk, and said, "Be careful."

"Too late, Mom," Regan had replied.

"Anyway," Luke continued, "yesterday I mentioned what you were doing to Austin. He reminded me we had heard last year about this girl who inherited money from her elderly neighbor in Hoboken and then started a dating service."

"Yes?" Regan said, her investigative antennae roused.

"This woman left her a lot of money."

"Yes, I know."

"It turns out she didn't make too many friends after the woman died. She even stiffed the Connolly brothers, who had handled the funeral, when they held a charity drive. They said she was cheap and couldn't get out of town fast enough."

"Being cheap isn't a crime," Regan said, "though maybe it should be."

"True. But it made them wonder whether there was any undue influence with the neighbor . . ."

And here I am in her apartment. Could Lydia have anything to do with any part of what had happened? "Maybe I should call them," Regan said. "Do you have their number?"

"Yes," Luke said and read it to Regan. "For what it's worth."

"Nothing would surprise me," Regan said. "I'll see you tonight."

"Be careful. Really."

Regan smiled. "Right, Dad." When she hung up, she pulled on her robe and stepped out into the kitchen. Maldwin was just getting out the coffee cups.

"I'm sorry I didn't bring coffee to you, but I think we all slept in a bit today. It's just ready now."

"That's okay," Regan said. "I'm going to go back across the hall and take a shower. My things are all there."

"Take a cup with you."

"Thanks. Is Lydia up yet?"

"No. I will wake her momentarily. Her pedicurist is coming in to do her nails at ten o'clock."

I wish I had someone coming to rub my feet, Regan thought. "Tell her thanks for me and I'll talk to her later."

Maldwin poured a cup of perfectly brewed coffee. "Milk and sugar?"

"Just some milk. I tell you, Maldwin, maybe you should start a butler school where I live in California."

Maldwin dropped the pitcher on the counter. "Excuse me," he said nervously.

"What's the matter? Don't you like California?" Regan teased.

"Too much sunshine," he said, pouring another cup and placing it on Lydia's tray.

What's he so worried about? Regan wondered as she walked across the hall, unlocked the padlock with the key the police had given her, and stepped back into what she now thought of as the abyss.

Dolly and Bah-Bah looked like two forlorn and forgotten figures in the corner of Jacques Harlow's loft. Movie equipment was all over the place. Up in his bed, which you had to climb a ladder to get to, Jacques was snoring like a jackhammer. They had filmed very late the previous night. The cast and crew were due back at noon.

Gray light filtered its way through the large, dirty windows, and the clock on the stove read 9:59.

The strident honk of the buzzer, indicating a visitor downstairs on the sidewalk, cut through the air. Several long honks later it finally penetrated Jacques's consciousness and woke him up. He jumped out of bed and pressed the intercom.

"What?" he growled.

"Good news, boss." It was one of his assistants, a squirmy little guy named Stewie, who had ambitions of Hollywood greatness.

"It better be good news. You woke me up."

"Buzz me in."

Jacques leaned on the button, specially installed next to his bed, and then descended the ladder. He walked over to the door and opened it just as Stewie was coming up the steps, bags with coffee and bagels in one hand, the newspaper in the other.

"Extra, extra, read all about it," Stewie sang as he walked through the door and handed the *New York World* to Jacques.

"Read all about what?"

"The Settlers' Club's problems. A side article talks about our flick and how the club was used as a location."

"*My* flick."

"Whatever." Stewie put the bags on the coffee table.

Jacques read for a minute, then threw the paper down. "Since when are you the producer?"

"I told her I was in production."

Jacques rolled his eyes and lifted the paper up again. "Ah, here I am!

"'The unpredictable and innovative director Jacques Harlow has his actors improvise their way through the story. It has been reported that two stuffed sheep belonging to the deceased club member, Nat Pemrod, became a part of the plot and were taken out of the club to be used at the next location.

"'Thomas Pilsner, president of the club, whose girlfriend retrieved food from the apartment of Ben Carney, another deceased member, was upset that the sheep were taken without his permission. Perhaps his girlfriend would like to make leg of lamb of them.'"

"Here's your coffee."

Jacques took a sip. "It's a good thing we took those sheep from the club. Otherwise we might not have rated a mention in the story."

"It's a good thing I found the club," Stewie said as he strutted around the loft. When he passed Dolly and Bah-Bah, he gave Bah-Bah a thump on the head. He didn't notice that one of Bah-Bah's eyes fell out and rolled away somewhere underneath the heater. "Boss, something tells me we should get through the shooting today and head up to that party tonight. Something tells me that's going to be where the action is. We could get more publicity." He paused. "Why are you staring off into space like that?"

"Something tells me we should do whatever we can to hang on to those sheep. They can be our logo for the company. It'll be called Two Sheep Productions."

"Should we try and buy them?"

"I think so."

"What if they don't want to sell them?"

Jacques looked at him harshly. "We'll make them an offer they can't refuse."

55

All over town, people were reading about the Settlers' Club. Lydia's ex-beau, Burkhard Whittlesey, was particularly enjoying the article as he rode a stationary bicycle at the cheapest, smelliest gym in New York City. It was all he could afford at the moment. But he was determined to get back in Lydia's good graces, so he had to keep in shape. She was his best shot at a decent life. I should have treated her better, he thought. I got a little too cocky.

Of course, in the long run, he considered himself much better suited to an aristocratic type. After all, he was a good-looking guy with a certain amount of charm. That's why he kept crashing all the high-class gatherings in town. He was always on the prowl for a bigger, better deal.

Since college, he'd managed to get himself on every party list going. He'd also mastered the art of dropping in at the cocktail hour of big benefits held in hotels, cruising around in his tux to see if there was anyone worthwhile, and then disappearing when it came time to take your seat. If he met anyone, he'd claim he had someplace else to go, but could they get together another time? But so far nothing had stuck. Every woman of means quickly figured out that he by no means had any means.

If Burkhard had put half the effort into working at a real job that he put into finding someone to take care of him, he might have been president of a Fortune 500 company. But every job he'd had started out with great promise and then imploded. Stocks he recommended tanked, deals he put together fell apart. Now at age thirty-five he was beginning to worry about his future. His roommate—whose name was on the lease of their dingy one-bedroom cockroach palace—had decided to join a commune in New Mexico. In a matter of weeks, Burkhard would be out on the street.

As he read the newspaper, he rode the bicycle faster and faster. That club certainly has its problems. It's going to be quite a scene tonight, he thought. I don't care what Lydia says. I'll go and turn on the charm for her. Show her what an asset

I can be. If she doesn't take the bait, I'll make a point of wandering over to any reporters who show up.

At the very least, she'll write me a check to keep my mouth shut.

Burkhard got up from the bicycle and walked to the showers. The sight of woolly-looking mold festering on the drain was too much for him. He went to his locker and threw on his sweat suit. I'll shower when I get home, he decided. Then I'll take a little walk around Gramercy Park, to prepare myself psychologically for tonight.

Lydia was his last shot before he'd have to move back to his parents' house in the sticks and take a job chopping firewood. He had no intention of letting that happen.

As he exited the "health" club and finally breathed some fresh air, he smiled. It'll be a benefit tonight. He laughed to himself. A benefit to benefit Burkhard Whittlesey.

56

Regan had just finished dressing when the doorbell rang. Here we go, she thought. It was Clara.

"Thomas told me to come upstairs and see you," Clara said anxiously, stepping inside.

"I've got to go talk to him. Do you know if he's seen the paper today?"

"He's a mess," Clara declared emphatically. "And that girlfriend of his is crying her eyes out."

"She is?" Regan said.

"Wouldn't you?" Clara answered, raising her arms in the air. "Thanks to that article people think this place is a tacky madhouse."

Regan just looked at her.

"All right, I'll admit calling in to that program

wasn't such a good idea. At least they didn't mention that in the paper."

"There's always tomorrow."

"Regan!"

"Sorry, Clara. I wanted to talk to you about Nat for a few minutes."

"Poor man."

"You heard about the break-in here last night?" Regan led her into the living room.

"Thomas told me. Would you look at this mess! Nat loved his books, and now they're thrown all over." Clara shook her head. "It's terrible. And those sheep. They were in this living room for so long. Now they're out of the building at that crazy movie set. Daphne had no right to let those weirdos take them away."

"She promised they'd be back tonight."

"She still had no right. They were Nat and Wendy's babies."

"How long have you worked here, Clara?"

"Ten years next Sunday."

"So you knew both Nat and his wife?"

Clara nodded. "A darling couple. A little too crazy about sheep for my taste, but to each his own."

"Thomas told me that Wendy was from England and had grown up in the country where there were a lot of sheep."

"Yeah, so, I grew up next to a dog pound. You don't find me with a bunch of stuffed dogs cluttering up my apartment."

Regan didn't argue the point. "They must have been perfect for each other then."

"You know what their song was?" Clara asked Regan. 'I Only Have Eyes for You.' That's *E-W-E*. Nat used to sing it to her all the time. They'd laugh and laugh." Clara's voice became softer. "He loved to play practical jokes. He definitely liked to have fun."

"Clara, did you see any sign that Nat had a girlfriend in this past month?"

Clara looked thoughtful. "You know, Regan," she said as she started walking down the hall, Regan following her, "he did buy a few new clothes about three weeks ago. He came in with a bunch of shopping bags, and he'd gotten a haircut and a shave at the barber's. He told me he hadn't gone out for a shave in years. He laughed and said the barber went to town on him, clipping his nose hairs and pruning his eyebrows. But then one day last week, as he was leaving, I asked if he was going out to get his nose hairs clipped, just kind of making a joke, and he said he didn't need to bother with silly things like that anymore."

That must have been when he decided to

break up with her, Regan thought. "But he didn't tell you anything about a girlfriend?"

"No! He might have felt funny, because all he did before that was talk about Wendy. Almost as if she were still alive. Come to think of it, for a few weeks there, he didn't say a thing about her, but then last week it was Wendy this and Wendy that again. I don't think he ever got over losing her."

Clara paused at the door to the master bedroom. "After she died, he wanted to keep everything the same. I'm not surprised it didn't last if he did take up with someone new." She then wandered over to the bathroom. "He had this all redone for her." All of a sudden she gestured wildly with her arm. "That's what it is, Regan!"

"What?"

"Wendy's towels are missing!"

"Wendy's towels?"

"Yes. They always hang on the rack over there." Clara pointed to the empty rack on the wall. "With the shock of it all yesterday, I didn't think of it. Nat never used those towels, but he always wanted them there. Occasionally I'd wash them, just so they'd look fresh."

"Did they have the sheep appliqué on them?" Regan asked.

"Of course."

"I found one of those appliqués on the floor by the shower," Regan said.

"They're very delicate. It must have fallen off."

So the towels are missing, Regan mused, and one of the appliqués was found by the shower. "Why would someone take the towels the night Nat died?" she asked aloud.

Clara looked befuddled. "And don't forget, on that night Nat takes a bath, not a shower. That's what he always took. A shower. Between ten and ten-thirty every night, he told me."

"So if he did take a shower that night, and whoever came in here wanted to make it look as if he'd slipped in the tub, they would have had to dry off the shower stall in case Nat was found before it dried off by itself. So they grab the towels in a hurry and rub vigorously—"

"And the sheep falls off!" Clara blurted out, finishing Regan's sentence. "Nat must have been murdered!"

"Clara, you've got to keep an eye out for those towels. Whoever took them might have hidden them somewhere in the club."

"A murderer was here, Regan! A murderer!"

"Clara, we don't know that."

"Yes we do. Why else would those towels be missing?"

Good question, Regan thought. "Clara, please don't call—"

"I'm not calling the crime show. Don't worry! But I'll search every inch of this club, looking for those towels." Clara clutched Regan's hand. "I want to help you find who did this to Nat. I'm telling you. He made my job easy. The man hated to take a bath!"

At New Scotland Yard, Jack was unsuccessful in finding anything that meant anything in the pile of papers, pictures, and maps found in the suspect's apartment.

His friend Ian finally suggested, "Why don't we wrap up here and go across to Finnegan's Wake for some lunch?"

Jack looked at his watch. It was already after two. There was a 6:00 P.M. flight he could catch home. "Sounds good," he said. I'll call Regan on my way to the airport, he thought.

At a corner table in the pub, they ordered pints of beer and shepherd's pie.

"So you don't want to stay and make a night of it here, Jack?" Ian asked him. "We could go out and have some fun."

Jack shook his head and smiled. "Thanks, Ian, but I've got to get back."

"Something tells me it's not for business," Ian said with a glint in his eye.

Jack took a sip of his beer. "Not really business, no." He told Ian about his relationship with Regan and what she was doing that weekend at the Settlers' Club. "It's funny, there's somebody running a butler school out of an apartment there. I mentioned it to the maid in my hotel here, and she said there's a lot of competition among the butler schools here."

Ian rolled his eyes. "It's more than friendly competition. We have one guy we're keeping an eye on. Thorn Darlington. He runs the biggest butler school, and he's trouble."

"Why?"

"He thinks he's the only one in this country, or the world for that matter, who should teach butlers how to serve tea. Most other schools that have opened over here have shut down. Usually under suspicious circumstances. The owner of one died in a late-night car crash. Another school burned down when a grease fire started in the kitchen. Yet another school's students all came down with food poisoning. A few of them nearly died. Needless to say, it was impossible for the school to find anyone new who would enroll there.

But Darlington's school always remains untouched."

"You think he was involved in the incidents?"

"Let's just say his name is written all over them, but we can't prove anything. We've heard he wants to open a butler school in New York now."

Jack frowned. "The butler school at the club is across the hall from the apartment where Regan is staying."

"I'd be interested to hear about it," Ian said. "Who knows whether this Thorn Darlington has gotten wind of it?"

Jack suddenly felt uncomfortable. "I'm glad I'm getting back today."

"If my girl were in a situation like that, I'd certainly want to get back there."

"It's not that she can't take care of herself . . ." Jack began.

Ian held up his hand. "I understand—when you love somebody . . ."

"Love somebody? I didn't say . . ."

"You didn't have to. Now I'll get the bill and go back to the office and run a check on Thorn Darlington's recent activities. You go get your things from the hotel, and I'll have a car pick you up in a half-hour to take you to the airport. I'll give the driver any information I have on Darlington."

"Thanks, Ian."

"Not at all. Next time you come over, bring this Regan Reilly. I'd like to meet her."

"I will," Jack said. More than ever, he felt restless, eager to get back home.

58

It didn't take long for Jack to pack his things in the hotel room. He dialed Regan's number on his cell phone. It rang three times before she picked up.

"Hey there," he said after she picked up.

"Jack. Hi." Regan's voice sounded relieved.

"What's the matter?"

"Where do I start? Well, let's see. Someone came into the apartment last night when I was sleeping. They ran away when they realized I was here."

Jack's hand squeezed the phone tightly. "I had a bad feeling about that place."

"And now I'm pretty convinced that Nat Pemrod was murdered."

"I'm on my way back," Jack told her.

"You are?" Regan's voice lightened.

"I've finished here. And I found out something that might just add to the troubles at that club. A guy named Thorn Darlington, who heads the most famous butler school in England, is planning to open a school in New York. He doesn't take kindly to anyone who tries to compete with his business."

"Oh, great," Regan said. "Maldwin will be thrilled to hear the news."

"They're getting more information on him for me. In the meantime, be careful around there."

Regan smiled. She hadn't told him the special significance that expression had for her. She'd wait till he got back. "I will. And I have other stories for you that you wouldn't believe. Yesterday really took the cake. This morning the Settlers' Club and all its woes are splashed on the front page of the *New York World*."

Jack sighed. "I'm really glad I'm coming back tonight."

"Me too. You know we have the club's anniversary party."

"Save me a dance."

Regan laughed. "A lot of Lydia's singles will be here. I'm sure the women will make a beeline for you."

"Thanks but no thanks. I'll tell them my dance card is full."

The maid knocked on Jack's door, then a half a second later, flung it open. "Oh, hello, love," she said.

"It sounds like your dance card is already full," Regan said.

"Very funny. I'll see you tonight."

Regan turned off her phone and smiled. Clara came up behind her. "Was that your boyfriend?" she asked.

"Yes," Regan said, although she'd never called him that.

"Ya know, you've got the same look on your face that Nat got when he talked about Wendy."

Oh, great, Regan thought. Let's hope I don't end up dead.

59

Maybe we should just break up." Janey cried daintily into her oatmeal.

Thomas grabbed her hand. "We could try counseling."

"Counseling? Why do we need counseling?"

"Because you want to break up."

"No I don't. I'm upset because I embarrassed you."

"Forget it! We'll get through this. Now eat, you need to eat." Thomas dug into his soft-boiled egg. "We need our strength to get through today."

"If only Mrs. Buckland hadn't called me yesterday wanting some stupid roast chicken. This never would have happened."

"Janey," Thomas chided, "life is full of 'if onlys.' If only Ben hadn't died, if only Nat hadn't died, if only they'd given us the diamonds before they died . . ."

"Hello, folks." Regan was standing at their table.

"Regan!" Thomas looked up. "Sit down."

"For a few minutes," Regan said as she took a seat. They were at the same table as the night before, and the dining room once again resembled a tomb. But tonight, Regan thought, hopefully, there will be some action. She glanced up at the portrait of the club's founder and was sure the expression on his face had turned into a scowl overnight. I can't blame him, she thought. "I saw Clara."

"The other troublemaker," Janey remarked.

"Don't do this to yourself, my darling. Clara was worse," Thomas insisted. "She broadcast our problems to the world. You didn't know that when you went over to Ben's and took the food that—"

"Thomas, I know what I did!"

Regan helped herself to a croissant and sipped the cup of coffee the waiter put in front of her. She didn't want to get in the middle of any tiff between the two lovebirds.

"I know you know," Thomas said. "All I'm saying is that you didn't know it would end up on the front page of the paper."

"Forget the paper," Regan advised.

"Have you seen it?" Thomas asked.

"No. My mother called me about it."

Janey groaned. "I could kill Mrs. Buckland." Then her face took on a startled expression. "She must be reading about it too! My business very well might go down the tubes!"

"Join the crowd," Thomas said wryly.

"Okay, now," Regan said. "I want to go out to the store and get those perfumes. Are you going to be around here later this morning, Janey?"

She nodded. "I'll be helping Thomas blow up balloons for the party tonight."

There's one way for the two of you to get rid of all your tension, Regan thought. After you're finished, you can hit each other in the head with them. "The police will be checking out the list Lydia gave me of people who were at the party. If you can match any of the perfumes I find to the one you smelled yesterday, we'll take it from there."

Thomas looked worried.

"What's the matter?" Regan asked.

"This morning Janey had the sniffles. Her nose is stuffed up. Probably from sitting on the floor of that cold closet all afternoon yesterday. Janey, after breakfast I'll get you some vitamin C."

"I won't be gone long," Regan said. "With any luck your sense of smell will hold out until I get back."

"I'll do my best," Janey said. Then her face brightened. "I just thought of a line I've always loved."

"What's that?" Regan asked.

"A rose by any other name would still smell as sweet."

"Beautiful," Regan muttered. And then she thought of the name of the perfume she was particularly taken by. Lethal Injection. I can't wait to see the bottle that stuff comes in, she thought.

◆

60

At the 13th Precinct, Detective Ronald Brier greeted Regan like an old friend. She had called ahead to see if he'd be there. The *New York World* was on his desk.

"I understand you had quite a night."

"Oh yes." Regan nodded and pointed to the newspaper. "Wait till that reporter finds out about the little visit to Nat's apartment last night."

"She already has."

"Already?"

"She came by this morning and was digging around for recent incidents in Gramercy Park. Boy, was she shocked when she read in the reports about what happened to you."

"Oh, great," Regan said.

"I know. But I've got some good news. They're doing a rush job on the fingerprints that we lifted from Ben Carney's and Nat Pemrod's apartments last night."

"What about the red box the diamonds were in?"

He shook his head. "They're working on it. But it looks like all the prints are smudged."

Regan pulled several lists out of her purse. "Here are the names of the people who were guests at the singles party, the student butlers, and everyone who lives and works at the club, including Lydia Sevatura, the woman who owns the dating service. There was some question about her after she received this windfall from her neighbor in Hoboken. I was hoping you could check it out."

Brier took the list from her. "You don't have a social security number or date of birth for her either, so it will take time. But she did rent the Settlers' Club apartment, so we'll be able to find out something."

"There's even more of a reason to check those names out other than the break-ins," Regan explained. "I'm really beginning to believe that Nat Pemrod was murdered."

Brier looked at her.

"I know that no one thought so the other night.

But a lot of things are suspicious. First the diamonds owned by Nat and Ben were missing. Then the break-ins at both Nat's and Ben's apartments. Now the maid tells me that not only did Nat never take a bath, but special appliquéd towels that he never used, because they belonged to his dead wife and he didn't want to ruin them, are also missing."

"Towels are missing?" Brier asked.

"According to the maid, Nat took a shower every night. Maybe the killer used the towels to dry the stall so if Nat was found in the bathtub not too long after he died, it wouldn't be suspicious that the shower was all wet."

"We didn't have any indication that this was anything but an accident. With all the people, including our cops, who have traipsed through there since Pemrod was found dead, any crime scene would be tainted. I think the chance of getting relevant physical evidence is nil."

"I know. Let's see what we can get from that list. In the meantime, I have a couple of other leads to work on."

61

Georgette was restless. Blaise had gone off to his butler class, and she was left to twiddle her thumbs until the evening, when she'd head over to the party. There was no money for shopping, and she didn't have the energy to do her rounds of the coffee shops.

Life was bleak.

She turned on the television in their little studio and started cleaning up. If only we had gotten those diamonds, she thought. On the counter were the four glass stones that had been in Nat's red box. She was about to throw them in the garbage, but something made her pick them up and hold them in her palm.

Sitting back down on the bed, she closed her hand over the stones and started to chant. Not that she was a real chanter. This was a chant she made up. Over the years, she'd visited psychics and had a mild interest in enlightenment. She thought that by chanting right now she might get a message about the location of the real diamonds.

"Ummmmm," she chanted in a singsong voice, closing her eyes. "Ummmmm."

No message so far.

She opened her eyes and stared at the glass stones. Nothing. She shut her eyes even tighter, leaned back and cried, "Ummmmmmmmm."

"Ummmmm" turned to "owwwww" when she banged her head against the cinderblock wall. Rubbing her bruised cranium, she pulled up the teddy bear that had been with her through thick and thin—lately mostly thin—and gave it a hug.

"Buttercup, what are we going to do?" She smiled when she thought about how she'd told Nat to call her Buttercup. He was a really nice old guy. Better than the one down in Florida who got nasty and called the cops when he caught her taking some jewelry. She hightailed it out of there fast. But Nat was sweet. Just the way he loved those sheep meant he had a good soul.

Georgette held out her teddy bear. "He had Dolly and Bah-Bah, and I have you."

The teddy bear stared back at her. It was so old that one of its eyes was gone.

"My poor baby." Impulsively, Georgette took one of the round glass stones and stuck it in the eye socket. It looked good! "There, that's better. I'll have to get some glue." She started to get up when an image flashed through her mind. She screamed again, but this time it was definitely not a chant.

"Dolly and Bah-Bah!" she cried, staring at the glass stones in her hand. "These are the eyes of Dolly and Bah-Bah! That's where the diamonds are!" She slammed her hand down on the bed, thinking of Nat's favorite song, "I Only Have Eyes for You." *Ewe!*

"Isn't that just like Nat?" She raced for her cell phone and called Blaise's. She got his voice mail. "He's probably learning how to change a lightbulb properly," she hissed. When his message ended, she practically spat into the phone. "I know where the diamonds are! Call me back before we're too late!"

62

Thorn Darlington was tired and irritable by the time he got off the plane at Kennedy Airport. Archibald had arranged for a car to pick him up. The driver was waiting, holding up a sign that said simply, COUSIN THORN.

How amusing of Archibald, Thorn thought sarcastically. He waved and walked over to the driver.

"Cousin Thorn?" the driver asked.

"To some people. Let's get my bags."

Fifteen minutes later, Thorn was settled in the back of a stretch limousine on his way into Manhattan. "Driver," he said, "a little privacy, please?"

The driver nodded and pressed a button, raising the glass partition between them. Thorn then pulled out his international cell phone and dialed. As usual, he got the voice mail on the other end.

"I hope we're ready for tonight," he said. "I'll be across the street at Cousin Archibald's. His superiority is so annoying. He thinks I'm here to celebrate the demise of the Settlers' Club thanks to him. Little does he know I have my own plans for the home of the Maldwin Feckles School for Butlers! Call me back!"

Thorn turned off his phone and giggled.

This is so perfect, he thought. My family was always much more cunning than Cousin Archie's.

63

Regan looked in the Yellow Pages and found a perfume shop off Seventh Avenue, near the site of the crime convention, called Our Scents Make Sense. "We carry every brand you can think of," the ad proclaimed. "Come take a whiff."

"I'm on my way," Regan announced to no one in particular. She grabbed a cab outside the club and found herself standing in front of a little hole-in-the-wall establishment with numerous perfume bottles lining the tiny storefront window. She opened the door, and bells that were taped to the other side tinkled, signaling her arrival.

A sixtyish woman with platinum-blond hair teased into helmetlike proportions was standing behind the long counter to the left. Even from six feet away, it was easy to spot that she had on the thickest, blackest eyeliner Regan had ever seen. Her outfit was a leopard jumpsuit, and her nails were three inches long. She must have gotten the job here when *Cats* closed, Regan thought.

Not surprisingly, the air in the tiny shop was filled with scents fighting with each other for domination.

"Hello, dahlink," the woman said to Regan. "How can I help you?" Her name tag read SISSY.

"Hello." Regan had the list in her hand. "There are about seven perfumes here I'd like to buy."

"Perfect, dahlink. One for every day of the week."

"Right," Regan said, thinking that Sissy's accent was of indeterminate origin. "The first one is called Ocean Water."

"Beautiful. Beautiful outdoor scent." She stepped away and pulled a bottle off the shelf. "There's Sunday." She smiled. "What about Monday?"

"Express to Passion."

"The best. That might be too much for a Monday!" she laughed as she reached for it and put it on the counter. "Next."

"Daisy Dewdrops."

Sissy made a face. "You sure you want that? A pretty young girl like you? It's so old-fashioned."

"I'm sure," Regan said. It was the perfume

Miss Snoopy Purse had been wearing. No wonder she'd been complaining about the others.

"Okay."

Within a minute they had nearly filled out the week with the scents Regan was looking for.

"Quite a variety," Sissy remarked. "That is good. Keeps a man on his toes."

If Jack could see me now. Regan smiled as she imagined his reaction. "The final one is Lethal Injection."

Sissy's eyes opened wide, even under the weight of her makeup, and she giggled. "You are a naughty girl."

Good God, Regan thought.

"Do you have a boyfriend?" Sissy asked as she reached for the bottle.

Regan felt sacreligious even talking to this woman about Jack. She nodded her head.

"He will love this," Sissy whispered conspiratorially. "It's very strong. A lot of men have come in here to buy it for their women."

Regan picked up the bottle and looked at it. It was in the shape of a thick black needle.

Sissy pulled off the cap. "You just push the needle like you're giving someone a shot, and out it sprays."

"Lovely," Regan muttered. "I wonder what genius came up with that idea."

"I don't know, but it's brand new!" Sissy said.

"It's brand new?" Regan repeated.

"They brought it out in time for Valentine's Day this year." She paused. "What's wrong?"

Regan shook her head, thinking of that woman, Georgette, who said her ex-boyfriend had given it to her. If he gave it to her recently, then why was she going to Lydia's parties? "Oh, nothing's wrong," she said. "How much do I owe you?"

Sissy rang it up. "Four hundred and twelve dollars and thirty-seven cents, tax included," she announced joyfully as she tore off the register tape.

I really hope we find those diamonds, Regan thought as she handed over her credit card. Or else I can just kiss this money good-bye. She signed the receipt and put the card back in her wallet.

"Thank you, dahlink," Sissy said as she dropped her business card in the shopping bag, handed it over to Regan, and winked. "Come back soon and tell me which day of the week your boyfriend likes best."

"Thank you," Regan said, with all the politeness she could muster, before fleeing the scene.

◆

64

Stanley was in his gas station–turned–apartment having a very exciting morning. The *New York World* was spread out in front of him. His tapes of the parties at Lydia's were on the couch. Maldwin had phoned to tell Stanley about the break-in at Nat's apartment in the middle of the night.

"I thought it was only fair to let you know," Maldwin said. "I still hope you'll concentrate on the butler school and Lydia's parties in your special. It means a lot to us."

"I will," Stanley had assured him.

Now his tapes might be more valuable than ever! I'm so grateful, he thought. I have truly been blessed. To have all these disasters happening at the club when he was the reporter on the scene! It was a very lucky break, a break many journalists never experienced in their lifetime. And he'd be there tonight for the one hundredth anniversary party, recording history again.

It was a good thing Maldwin wrote to him about the butler school. Stanley wanted to review the interviews he'd done the night before with the four student butlers.

He popped the tape in the VCR and pressed PLAY. The first student interviewed was that dreadful Vinnie. Stanley could not imagine for the life of him who would hire Vinnie as their butler. He was disrespectful and didn't seem to care in the least about gracious living. He must be paying off a bet, Stanley thought. I wouldn't hire him to be the butler for the gas station, let alone a country estate.

Next up was the handsome Blaise. He looked like a soap-opera star. He certainly has that aloof, remote quality that Hollywood portrays so many butlers as having, Stanley thought. Is he putting on an act?

"I like to devote myself completely to what I do," Blaise said into the camera. "And I know that butlering can be a 24/7 job. I look forward to it."

What a crock, Stanley thought.

Harriet came into view, smiling that saintly smile. "Oh, wow," she began. "It's always been my dream to be a butler. But I never thought I'd be able to. Thank goodness I live in a time where women are finally being accepted as butler students. I say that women have a natural instinct for taking care of a home, and I will channel that instinct into my devoted services as a butler. Thank you soooooo much."

Who could put up with that Pollyanna sweetness all the time? Stanley wondered. It gets grating.

Finally there was Albert, who couldn't seem to wipe the goofy expression off his face. "I enjoy the finer things in life and know that I'd never be able to afford them. So I thought, Why not be a butler? Then you can be surrounded by beauty and help take care of it too. I used to work in a video store, and when they started renting out pornography, I said, 'That's it! It's too disgusting for me!' The next day I signed up for Maldwin's class and the rest is history."

Not exactly an inspiring bunch, Stanley observed. But with a little music in the background and proper editing, he could do right by Maldwin. Maldwin deserved that much.

With all the confusion of the movie company shooting yesterday, Stanley hadn't had much of a chance to film the park in its peaceful state. The movie trucks had been parked all over. I'll go up there now, he thought. Thomas had said to get to the club early and film the preparations for the party. He could change in Thomas's apartment.

Stanley packed his tapes and his camera in a bag. His dark suit was pressed and ready to go. This is going to be exciting, he thought.

Who knows what direction my special is going to take?

65

Thomas and Janey were in his office, surrounded by dozens of floating balloons. Thanks
to the newspaper story, calls had been coming in
from various shows and news organizations, asking for Thomas's comments. Some of the callers
wanted to come to the party. But Thomas
refused every one of them. He knew what their
intentions were.

Make the Settlers' Club look bad.

He had decided that only Stanley would be
allowed in. If the club was going to go to hell in a
handbasket, at least it would be done with dignity. That true-crime show even had the nerve to
call the club and ask for Clara. He'd put the kib-
bosh on that immediately.

"Any calls to Clara must go through me," he instructed the front desk.

"What about her sister?"

"Especially her sister! That woman has blabbermouth soup for lunch," Thomas declared.

"Okay, boss. We've got Mr. Pemrod's lawyer on the other line. Do you want to speak to her?"

"Of course I do! Put her through."

Katla McGlynn was in her office, having stopped in after an early round of golf. She lived and worked in Westchester and had started doing Nat's legal work after buying a necklace from him over twenty years ago. In her early fifties, Katla had a small practice that catered to the varied needs of her clients.

"Hello!" Thomas practically yelled into the phone.

"Mr. Pilsner?"

"Speaking."

"My name is Katla McGlynn. I'm Nat Pemrod's lawyer. I just read about his death and the missing diamonds. I feel terrible about Nat. He was a good guy."

"He was," Thomas agreed, tapping his foot.

"I just want you to know that I received a letter in the mail today that Nat and Ben Carney wrote on Thursday, declaring their intention to donate those diamonds to the club."

Thomas nearly fainted again. "You did?"

"Yes. In case the diamonds are found, you should have a copy of the letter."

"Did you know about the diamonds before?" Thomas asked.

"No. Nat never mentioned them to me. The only thing he joked about was those sheep of his. He said they were to go into the parlor of the club when he died. Are they there now?"

"It's a long story," Thomas said.

"I've got time. I am the executor of his estate. I want to see that his wishes are followed."

"There was a movie company here yesterday . . ."

"I read about them."

"Well, you see, apparently they used the sheep in a scene and took them to the next location without asking my permission. They'll be back tonight."

"I hope so. Any guy who was willing to donate such a generous gift should have his wishes honored, no matter what happens."

"I couldn't agree more," Thomas said emphatically.

"I'll be down on Monday to start handling everything." She gave Thomas her number. "Call me if you need anything between now and then."

"Okay."

As soon as Thomas hung up, the phone rang again.

"It's Daphne, calling from the movie set."

"Put her through!"

"Thomas, it's Daphne."

"Bring those sheep back right now!"

"I've got great news! They want to buy the sheep for their movie company!"

"No!"

"Please."

"No!"

"They're willing to pay a lot of money."

"I don't even want to know how much. Nat's lawyer just called. She wanted to make sure Dolly and Bah-Bah are where Nat wanted them. And that's in the front parlor in their own home, the Settlers' Club."

"But Nat would have wanted it this way. And I was always so good to him after Wendy died. If the Settlers' Club has to close down, it won't do us any good."

"Absolutely not. I have half a mind to come down to that set and pick them up right now. Where are you?"

The phone clicked in his ear.

66

Inside the Paisley Hotel, the morning sessions of the crime convention were just wrapping up. Kyle Fleming, the FBI agent from Florida, had given such an informative, albeit amusing lecture the day before on con artists, that he'd been asked to fill in for another speaker who canceled at the last minute. Fleming had always been fascinated by the number of people in the world who were crooks.

"Big-time crooks, small-time crooks, they're all out there just dying for your money," he'd said. "Some of them will do just about anything to get it. The people who interest me are not the ones who climb through a window and rob you blind. Anyone can try that. Anyone can steal your purse when you turn your back at the airport. It's the crooks who gain your trust, your confidence, and then rob you blind. That's what really hurts. So many of them get away with these crimes because people are too embarrassed to come forward with their stories.

"Con artists come in all shapes and sizes, and many of them are masters at changing their appearance so they're not easily detected. They move around, hit a target, and then they're gone. That's what makes them hard to catch.

"Here are a few of my favorites . . ."

He showed slides of several people and talked about each one.

"This smooth operator had several wives who obviously didn't know about each other. He bilked them of their savings and broke their hearts. He may not look like Romeo, but he obviously had something . . .

"This couple would blow into big cities, create an image of success by throwing lavish parties to which they'd invite people they barely knew, then get some of these same people who were impressed by it all to invest in their scams . . ."

Members of the audience asked so many questions that Fleming didn't get to all his slides. He'd been about to flash the photo of Georgette Hughes on the screen when he looked at his watch.

"This next one is a crook who is a master at changing her look, but I think she deserves ten minutes, and our time is up," he concluded.

The crowd groaned.

Nora stood. "I think it's safe to say that we'd all love for Kyle to continue. I certainly hope he'll join us again next year."

The crowd gave an enthusiastic round of applause as Nora went over to shake Kyle's hand. "Kyle, are you free tonight? I've invited a number of the people here to a cocktail party down at the Settlers' Club. It's their one hundredth anniversary. Then we'll go for a late dinner."

"Thanks, Nora," Kyle said. "I'll try to stop by. But I already have plans."

67

Regan walked past the Paisley Hotel and hesitated. She'd have loved to go inside and say hello to her mother and all the people she knew. She'd only gotten a chance to see them at the opening-night cocktail party, which seemed like weeks ago.

I'd better not take the time, Regan thought. I should really get back.

She hailed a cab, and fifteen minutes later was at the club.

"Miss Reilly," the guard greeted her. "Clara's looking for you."

Regan's heart skipped a beat. "Where is she?"

"In the parlor."

Regan hurried up the steps. Clara was by the fireplace, shining up the pokers and shovels that were strictly for show. Ever since they'd been smoked out thanks to a faulty flue, fake logs were the order of the day.

When Clara saw Regan, her eyes bugged out and she dropped the shovel she'd been working on. The din could be heard across the park. "Regan!" she exclaimed as she leaned down to pick it up.

"Are you all right?"

"I need to talk to you in private," Clara whispered.

They went up to Nat's apartment without running into anyone. Shutting the door behind them, Clara ran down the hall to the kitchen. "Look what I found!" she cried.

Sitting on the floor of the kitchen was a black trash-can liner. Clara yanked it open and pulled out a damp towel. "Wendy's towels!" she bellowed as she dropped the first one on the counter and pulled out the second one. "And it's such a shame. They're all smelly from sitting in this bag."

"Where did you find them?" Regan asked quickly.

"In the Dumpster out back."

"I thought you told me the Dumpster was emptied on Fridays."

"It is! Whoever left these must have dropped them in there after the garbageman left yesterday!"

"So that could have been last night or early this morning."

"Uh-huh," Clara nodded, and then, almost as if she were operating on automatic pilot, said, "It's such a pity. They're ruined. They stink and a couple of the sheep appliqués are gone. What good are the towels without them? And this trash-can liner must be Nat's. I told him on Thursday he'd better buy more, there was only one left. Look!" She opened the cabinet and triumphantly pulled out an empty box with a picture of a garbage can on it. "All gone!"

"Clara," Regan said incredulously "Did you go through the Dumpster?"

Clara looked guilty. "I've been so excited today that during my break I went out the back door for a smoke. I've quit at least ten times! Anyway, one of the waiters came out to throw some garbage away, and when he flipped open the Dumpster, I could see the peach color peaking through a rip in the bag."

"So you reached into the Dumpster?"

"You told me to be discreet, so I waited until he went back inside. When I saw it was Wendy's towels, I ran to get a laundry bag so I could throw the whole thing in there and carry it upstairs."

"Clara," Regan said, "you're amazing."

"Thank you, Regan. But Regan . . ."

"Yes, Clara."

"I'm a little scared."

Regan and Clara both stared at the soggy towels that Nat and Wendy had cherished. Towels that had most likely been used to cover up Nat's murder.

68

When Daphne hung up the phone, she was afraid to go back and tell Jacques that Thomas wouldn't sell the sheep to him. Be a good actress, she told herself. That's what counts.

She sashayed over to where Jacques had planted his director's chair. His cigarette holder was dangling out of his mouth, and his black beret was back in place.

"Well?"

Daphne laughed as though she didn't have a care in the world. "It turns out, Jacques, that the sheep have deep, deep meaning for the club."

"What do you mean 'deep meaning?'"

"I mean that they are an important part of the club's history, and they're not interested in selling them."

Jacques removed the cigarette holder from his mouth. "Don't you want parts in my movies? Starring roles?"

"Of course I do, Jacques. It's a privilege for me to work with you."

"Those sheep are magic," Jacques said, pointing to Dolly and Bah-Bah. "I don't know what it is about them, but they've got something special. *And I want them! I want, I want,* I WANT THOSE SHEEP! And you are the only one who can arrange that. So do it! Tell them we'll give them fifty thousand dollars." He turned away and flicked his hand. "Get a check from what's his name and take it up there now. Make sure they accept it!"

A moment later, Daphne took the check that had been hastily scrawled, raced down the steps to the street, and hightailed it up to the club as though her life depended on it.

69

Y̶ou may take a lunch break now," Maldwin announced to his little group of four.

"Thank you!" Harriet said cheerfully. "Can I bring anyone a sandwich from the deli?"

"No," said Albert.

"Nah," echoed Vinnie.

"I'm not very hungry," Blaise said as politely as he could. He felt like wringing Harriet's neck. She was like the kid in school who always reminded the teacher to give homework assignments.

"Okay," Harriet said, wrinkling her little pug nose. "Maldwin, I'll come back in a few minutes and do any extra work that might need doing around the apartment."

"Take the whole hour off," Maldwin urged her. Do me a favor, he thought. Do us all a favor.

Vinnie whispered to Albert, "Let's go get a beer. This is going to be a long day."

"Good thinking."

Blaise went over to Maldwin. "Do you think I could have the key to the park? I just want to sit outside."

"It's cold," Maldwin sniffed.

Blaise smiled. "I have a hat."

Maldwin shrugged. "Why not?" He went into the kitchen and retrieved the key that was only given to residents of Gramercy Park. The lock was changed every year, and residents had to pay to get a new key. On a cold day like today there'd hardly be anyone there, so who could complain about a nonresident using the park? "Enjoy the fresh air," he said, handing the key to Blaise.

Outside, Blaise went directly to the park and unlocked the gate. He was getting that feeling of claustrophobia he always experienced when things started closing in on him. It was cold and gray, but he needed to be outside. I want to go back to Florida, he thought, reaching in his coat pocket and pulling out the stretchy wool hat that he used when he went skiing. He looked around as he pulled it down over his hair. No one else was in the park.

He took a seat on the first bench and reached again into his pocket, this time for his cell phone.

Flipping it open, he saw that he had a message. Probably Georgette with a new complaint, he thought. He pressed in his code, and when he heard her news he jumped up out of his seat. Frantically he started pacing as he dialed her cell number. "Where are they?" he screamed when she answered.

"In the sheep's eyes!"

"What are you talking about?"

"Well, I was sitting here with Buttercup, feeling kind of sorry for myself, and then I leaned back and—"

"Get to the point!"

"The point is that those two stuffed sheep Nat has in his living room are where the diamonds are. These glass stones were in their eyes. He must have switched them."

"What a nut case."

"Don't I know it."

"Wait a minute. *Where* in his living room are the sheep?"

"Right in front of the window."

"No they're not."

"Yes they are."

"No they're not, my little Buttercup," Blaise repeated sarcastically. "They were absolutely not there last night."

"Well then, where are they?"

"How am I supposed to know?"

Georgette started to cry. "I feel like Little Bo Peep."

Blaise sat back down on the bench. "Yeah, well, her sheep weren't worth millions."

That remark made Georgette really sob.

"Listen," Blaise said in a comforting tone. "I'll go back in there and do my best to find out where they went." He didn't need Georgette falling apart. "Now dry your eyes and get dressed up for tonight. Because when we leave the party, something tells me we'll be walking out of there millionaires. You'd better stick the gun in your purse."

"Okay," Georgette said, nervously. "I guess we might need it."

"We'll need it if anybody tries to stop us." When he hung up, Blaise rolled his eyes. "Little Bo Peep," he said aloud.

He didn't know that Stanley had just walked up to the gate and was filming him.

Jack was grateful when his plane taxied down the runway and took off for New York. Time to get back, he said to himself. Time to get back.

Thorn Darlington was on his mind. Jack had found out right before he got on the plane that Darlington was headed to New York too and would be staying with relatives in Gramercy Park. Too close for comfort, he thought. He had called Regan one more time and told her.

Jack accepted a drink from the flight attendant and sat back. He tapped his fingers on the tray table, reached down into his bag, and pulled out a notebook and pen. He wanted to make a list of things that he had to get done.

But it was hard to concentrate. Every instinct he had told him that there was more trouble ahead at the Settlers' Club.

Silently, Jack prayed for the plane to go faster.

Archibald and Vernella and Cousin Thorn had been enjoying lunch at a portable table by the window in the living room when they noticed Blaise coming out of the Settlers' Club and going into the park. Because the Enderses had made it their business to know the names and faces of everyone who had a key to the park, they were immediately outraged.

"You see!" Archibald whined to Thorn, who was in the middle of helping himself to another piece of cake. "The Settlers' Club lets anyone use the park. And look at that man in that dopey orange hat, gesturing madly. He looks like a crazy person. I'm putting on my coat and going out there!"

"Jolly good," Thorn said, smacking his lips.

"We'll watch you, darling," Vernella said, clearly enjoying herself.

Archibald put on his coat and top hat, grabbed his walking stick, and exited the front door. He looked like a man going for his morning constitutional.

"This is like live theater," Vernella said, her eyes following Archibald as he approached the park and confronted the man with the hat who had had the gall to admit into the park a man with a video camera.

Four minutes later, Archibald strode back into his living room.

"Cousin Thorn, I have good news. That sorry individual was one of Maldwin's butler students!"

"One of Maldwin's butler students!" Thorn echoed. "It shows the caliber of his students, doesn't it? Not such serious competition!"

"This calls for a glass of sherry!" Vernella cried.

"I don't know whether we should celebrate so soon," Thorn said with trepidation. "It might be a while before we get the butler school out of there. We don't want to jinx our plan."

"Believe me, Cousin, we can celebrate," Archibald declared. "With all the negative publicity, no one will want to join that club. I will own that building before the buds are on the trees. So bring on the sherry!"

Vernella hurried to the sideboard and took out three small glasses. Archibald broke out his favorite bottle and poured it with great ceremony. "I propose a toast."

"Go ahead, sweetie," Vernella urged.

"To the end of tacky days in Gramercy Park and to the fall of the Settlers' Club. Let it be swift and sure."

They clinked glasses.

You'd better believe it, Thorn thought. You don't know how swift and sure. He looked across the street and pictured all the emergency vehicles with their flashing lights that would be racing to the Settlers' Club tonight.

He couldn't wait.

72

Regan had lined up the seven perfume bottles on Thomas's desk. Janey was sitting with her eyes closed, facing the other way. Regan didn't want her to be influenced by the names or packaging, and she wanted Janey to concentrate completely on her sense of smell.

"Ready?" Regan asked.

"Ready."

Thomas was sitting in the corner, biting his fingernails. It was a habit he had developed only yesterday.

Regan picked up the bottle of Daisy Dewdrops and sprayed it on a sheet of paper. May as well start slowly, she thought. An unlikely scent for a criminal, but you never know. She held the paper up to Janey's nose.

"That's beautiful," Janey sighed. "Could I have that bottle when we're finished?"

"Why not? But I guess that's not what we're looking for."

"No." Janey sat up a little straighter and gently wiped her nose with a tissue.

Regan sprayed Ocean Water on paper and held it up.

"Definitely not," Janey said.

Regan had been afraid to try the Lethal Injection because, in her heart, she knew it was the most likely candidate and she didn't want it to be rejected. After all, Georgette had lied to her. If a boyfriend had given her the perfume, it must have been recently. Had she really broken up with her boyfriend? If not, what was she doing at the singles parties?

Regan picked up the bottle, pushed the needle, which released the spray, and barely had the paper under Janey's nostrils when Janey cried out, "That's it! That's the perfume she was wearing!"

Thomas leaped from his chair, and the two of them engaged in another hug, similar to the one that took place when Janey was sprung from the closet yesterday.

"I knew you could do it," Thomas cried. "I'm so proud of you."

Regan looked at the lineup of the four

untouched bottles. I wonder if I can return those? Probably not, she thought wryly. The wrappers have been removed. She cleared her throat. "I'm going to go upstairs and talk to Lydia," she announced as the couple finally broke apart. And then I'll give Ronald Brier a call, she thought. Find out what, if anything, he has on Georgette.

73

I need to speak to both you and Lydia," Regan told Maldwin when he answered the door. "In private."

"Miss Lydia is resting up for tonight."

"This is important."

Maldwin could tell by her tone that she meant business. "Very well," he said and led her into the living room. "I will return shortly."

Regan sat and looked around at Lydia's new furnishings. This is all here because she inherited money from an elderly neighbor. I have to call those funeral directors Dad told me about, Regan thought.

A few moments later, Lydia came into the room looking visibly strained. Maldwin was right behind her.

"Hello, Regan," Lydia said.

"Lydia, are you feeling all right?" Regan asked.

"I'm just worried about tonight, that's all. All this negative publicity doesn't help." She didn't mention that she'd just received another call from Burkhard, who had told her to save a dance for him. His tone was so menacing it made her skin crawl. "I want it to go well," she added.

"We all do," Regan said simply.

Maldwin sat looking ill at ease. The last thing he needed was controversy. "I've given my students the task of rearranging the cabinets in the kitchen," he told Regan. "So we could be alone."

"Thank you," Regan said. "Now, there are a couple of things. Maldwin, do you know a Thorn Darlington?"

Maldwin blanched. "Yes."

"A friend of mine was just in London. Apparently, Thorn is on his way over to New York. For what reason, I don't know."

"Probably to destroy me," Maldwin said. "He's an evil man."

"He's staying somewhere in Gramercy Park." Maldwin gulped.

"What good news do you have for me, Regan?" Lydia asked with an edge to her voice.

"I just wanted to ask you about that woman Georgette who comes to your parties. What can you tell me about her?"

Lydia leaned forward and put her head in her hands. "Don't tell me she's not a quality single."

"There is something a little pushy about her," Maldwin offered, glad to turn the subject to other people's problems.

"What do you mean?" Regan asked.

"During the parties she would come into the kitchen, gather up a bunch of pigs in blankets, then five minutes later she'd be gone."

Regan's jaw tightened. She'd found pigs in blankets in Nat's garbage can.

"But she came to every party," Lydia countered. "Even if only for a little while."

And then disappeared across the hall, Regan thought. She's sounding more and more like our gal Buttercup. "You don't have an address for her, do you?" she asked Lydia.

"She didn't give me one. I value my singles' privacy, so I didn't push for it."

"Do you know if she'll be here tonight?" Regan asked.

"She told me she would come," Lydia answered.

Blaise was standing in the hallway, eavesdropping. Oh, she will, he thought. She'll come, but as someone else.

Around the corner, one of the other student butlers had also been listening. Wait till Thorn hears this, the student thought.

74

Absolutely not!" Thomas declared. "Daphne, you must bring back those sheep tonight!"

Daphne was standing in the doorway of his office. She stepped in, pushed a few balloons off a chair, and sat down. "Thomas, please! Here is a check for fifty thousand dollars!"

"I can't accept that. Nat would haunt the place."

"But it means so much to me and to my career! And the club needs the money! Nat owes me this much!"

"Daphne, the answer is *no!* Those sheep have been here for years, this is their home. It's what Wendy and Nat wanted for them. If the club goes out of business, the movie company can have them. But for now their home is here!"

"Fifty thousand dollars, Thomas!"

"That money is not going to make or break the club. Now I want you to bring home those sheep. They are to be here in time for the party, which starts at seven o'clock!"

Daphne stormed out, hot tears welling in her eyes. She nearly knocked Blaise off his feet in the hallway. "Excuse me," she mumbled and hurried off.

"Blaise," Thomas called.

"Yes, sir," Blaise said, appearing in the doorway.

"I got a call from our crazy neighbors complaining that Maldwin gave you the key to the park. I'm sorry, but it's not allowed."

Blaise smiled cheerfully. "I promise you it will never happen again."

75

Even though Thomas had been totally understanding, Jancy couldn't help but feel sick to her stomach about what she'd done. In the grand scheme of things, I suppose it's not so bad, she thought. But today she imagined that everyone in the world must be talking about her—the woman who was no better than a grave robber.

In the ladies' room on the first floor of the club, she looked at her reflection in the mirror. I've got to redeem myself, she thought. But how? She'd told Thomas that she was going home to gather up all the cakes and pies and cookies she'd baked for tonight. Although they're probably all stale by now, she thought with a pang of guilt. She ran a comb through her hair, picked up her coat and purse, and opened the door just in time to see Daphne storming by.

"When are you bringing back the sheep?" the guard asked Daphne.

"Not till I'm good and ready," Daphne cried.

Janey froze and watched Daphne fly out the door.

The guard shook his head and looked at Janey. "She'd better bring them back today. Thomas really wants them here for the party."

Through the glass panes on the front door, Janey could see Daphne jump in a cab. This is my chance for redemption, Janey thought, and ran outside. Another cab had just let out a fare next door. Janey flung her body into the backseat and yelled, "Follow them!"

76

Back in Nat's living room, Regan sat down on the couch, glad for a quiet moment, and turned on a table lamp. It was only three o'clock, but the room felt dim and gray. It was the kind of room on the kind of day where one would be inclined to curl up with a good book, a cup of tea, and a blanket. Maybe even take a nap. But not after last night. Regan shuddered. Or the night before. Now Regan had no desire to ever close her eyes in the place again. She didn't even want to let herself blink.

Clara had put all the books back on the shelves. The space in front of the window once occupied by the sheep was now empty. Thomas had said Nat and Wendy used to joke that Dolly and Bah-Bah were like their kids. They certainly had a place of honor in this room, Regan thought, the room where "the Suits" used to play cards.

Thomas had also mentioned to her that Nat and Ben told him that they'd bring the diamonds out of the safe during every card game and have some fun with them. They'd explained, "What good is having valuable diamonds all these years if you don't enjoy them in some way?" So what could you do with them that would be so much fun? Regan wondered.

She picked up the phone and called Detective Ronald Brier. When he answered, she told him about the towels and the perfume.

"So who wore the perfume?" he asked.

"Georgette Hughes."

"You don't have an address for her, right?"

"Right."

"And of course none of these people from the singles group gave a date of birth."

"It *is* a singles group," Regan said.

Brier checked his list. "We have nothing on her. The club employees were easy to look up since we had a social security number and date of birth for each of them. But the others are much more difficult."

"Okay," Regan said. "Georgette is going to be at the party tonight. I'll see what else I can find out."

"You're going back to California on Monday, aren't you?"

"Yes. And I'm afraid I'll be leaving without having been of much help on this case. It's all pretty frustrating."

"We'll keep digging," Brier assured her. "The prints take time, and we'll follow up on any leads from these lists."

"Ronald," Regan began.

"Yes?"

"Did you find anything on Lydia—the woman who owns the dating service?"

On the other end, Brier tapped his pen on the desk. "Not much. I called the funeral home. I'm sure you know how it is, Regan, with your father being in the funeral business. When someone dies there's a lot of gossip. Apparently, Lydia lived right across the hall from this woman, Mrs. Cerencioni. She'd show up with food, run errands for her, that kind of thing. Lydia would joke with her about how they should both find rich husbands. The policeman who arrived on the scene when Mrs. Cerencioni died said Lydia was very upset at the time. It was the neighbors in the building who were saying mean things." Brier laughed. "I think they were jealous the old lady didn't leave *them* any money."

"So that's all it was?"

"Regan, you never know. Maybe she did have a motive for being so kind. But no one knew how much money the old lady had. Who knows? Maybe Lydia had somehow found out and set her sights on the pot of gold at the end of the rainbow, as they say. Mrs. Cerencioni didn't have any relatives."

I guess there's no need for me to call the Connollys, Regan thought. "By the way," she said. "What did Mrs. Cerencioni die of?"

"She fell in the bathtub."

Oh, great, Regan thought. That's just great.

77

Janey felt a sense of empowerment. I'm going to bring those sheep back to the club myself, she thought. That's all there is to it.

From the backseat she instructed the cabdriver to change lanes several times.

"Okay, lady, okay," the driver shouted as he snapped his fingers to the music on the radio.

On a downtown street that looked as if it could use serious rehabilitation, Janey's cab pulled up behind Daphne's. Janey threw a few bills at the driver and jumped out, just catching the door that Daphne had run through before it shut and locked. Daphne dashed up the staircase to the second floor.

She moves fast, Janey thought. But so can I. Janey ran up the steps after her and caught up to her on the landing.

"Daphne!" Janey yelled.

Daphne hurled herself around with fire in her eyes. "What do you want, you little food grubber?"

"I'll choose to ignore that," Janey said politely. "You know what I'm here for. Dolly and Bah-Bah. It's time to bring them home."

"My career will be ruined if they have to leave," Daphne insisted.

"Well, I don't think my career is in such good shape at the moment either," Janey replied. "Everyone in New York knows that if they die before they eat my food, I'll be back to take it. How do you think that feels?"

"It's your own fault for being lazy," Daphne snapped.

"Once again, I'll turn the other cheek. But I'm going in with you to get the sheep."

Daphne rang the bell, and an assistant let them in. Pumpkin was standing alone in the middle of the set, doing stretches and making guttural noises as she prepared for the next scene. Janey could see that Dolly and Bah-Bah were positioned under the hot lights. They looked as if they'd been combed and brushed and fluffed.

"You're back!" Jacques cried to Daphne. "And who is this with you?"

"Hello, sir!" Janey said. "I'm from the Settlers' Club, and I'm here to get the sheep."

"What?!" Jacques demanded.

"I couldn't talk them into it," Daphne apologized. "I'm sorry."

Jacques shook his head. "Then get *out!* Both of you! Ruin my movie! Take them! I'll get new ones someplace else!"

"Are you firing me?" Daphne asked.

"I guess that's what you would call it."

As Daphne ran to grab the wardrobe she'd brought down with her in the morning, Janey hurried over and grabbed Dolly. One of Dolly's eyes popped out onto the floor. She quickly picked it up and stuck it back in, noticing that the other eye was also gone. She looked over at Bah-Bah and lifted up the wool off his face. He, too, was a one-eyed monster.

"Hurry up!" Jacques ordered. "Get out! I can't stand the sight of you!"

Janey began looking around on the floor for the missing eyes.

"Move!" Jacques cried.

"Their eyes are missing," Janey explained. "I have to find the two eyes!"

"You can get them another time. I have to make my movie."

The sense of empowerment Janey felt in the cab was firmly in place. "I'm not leaving until we find those eyes!"

"Help her find the eyes!" Jacques screamed. In an instant, several assistants were on their hands and knees, searching the floor.

"Pretty dusty down here," one of them muttered.

"I'm giving you thirty seconds," Jacques yelled. "Time is money."

From the corner, one of the assistants cried, "I found one! Under the heater!"

"And I found the other!"

The two assistants came from different directions and handed the eyes to Janey.

"GET OUT!"

Janey stuffed the stones in her coat pocket and grabbed Dolly under the belly. She turned and called to Daphne. But she was gone. "Could someone please help me carry this other one downstairs?" Janey asked. "I'd be ever so grateful."

At least six assistants tripped over themselves trying to help. Janey was down the steps and out on the sidewalk in two minutes, Dolly and Bah-Bah next to her. Not a cab nor a car was in sight. "Well, guys," Janey said as she reached in her purse for her cell phone. "I'll have to call a car service." Janey's newfound sense of empowerment continued its streak. "I have two very important passengers," she declared to the car service. "I'd like a limo. Make it a stretch!"

78

Back at the club, there was a flurry of activity. Stanley had his trusty video camera out, following the staff and student butlers around as they spit and polished, placed fresh flowers around the first-floor rooms where the party would be held, prepared food in the kitchen, and set up buffet tables. The whole downstairs area of the club had been cleaned and shined. Clara had worked like a dog all day long and was exhausted.

"Clara," Thomas said. "Why don't you stay for the party tonight?"

"You mean to work?" she asked incredulously.

"No, I mean to have a good time."

"That's different," she said.

"Do you have anything to wear?"

"I keep a dress and a nice pair of shoes in my

locker because sometimes my sister gets half-price tickets for the theater at the last minute, and I always want to be prepared, just in case—"

"Very good," Thomas said, cutting her off. "If you'd like to take a nap, you can go into my apartment and lie down on the couch."

"Are you feeling all right?" Clara asked, suspiciously.

"More than all right," Thomas shot back. "I've decided that if we're going down, we may as well enjoy our last moments."

Clara looked thoughtful. "It's kind of like one of those movies where you die and then you come back to life and enjoy things more."

"Something like that." Thomas stared out the front window of the club. "Oh my God," he said.

Clara followed his gaze. "The sheep are getting out of a stretch limo with Janey!"

"Now you see why I fell in love with her," Thomas said softly.

"Well, if you love her, you'd better go help her drag them in here."

Stanley appeared behind them. "What's going on?" he asked.

"Nat and Wendy's sheep are back," Thomas said as he hurried outside.

"I love this!" Stanley cried, capturing on film the limo and the sheep being carried over the threshold of the club. "I'm sure I'll be able to use this in my piece."

Thomas and Janey carried the sheep back into the parlor, Stanley's camera following their every move. "Thomas, if these sheep are so important, we should do something dramatic with them," he suggested. "It'd be good for my piece."

"What should we do?" Thomas asked. "I was going to put them in front of the fireplace."

Stanley shook his head and looked around. "Why don't we place them on a platform by the window? It'd be gorgeous. You know how some restaurants have all sorts of stuff hanging from the walls? The two sheep could be like two guards at Buckingham Palace, except they're guarding the Settlers' Club. And if they're up in the air like that, they'll be seen from the street."

"That sounds wonderful," Janey said. "We can put the big anniversary cake on a table between them."

"*You're* wonderful," Thomas declared. "You brought them back."

Clara rolled her eyes and said to Stanley, "Who are we going to get to build a platform?"

"I turned a gas station into a home. I can do it."

"Thomas," Janey said, "I'm going to run to my apartment and get the cakes and pies."

"If Mrs. Buckland calls, please don't answer the phone," Thomas called after her.

Janey laughed and bounced out of the room, the sheep's eyes jiggling in her coat pocket.

"Thomas," Stanley said, "I know just how to build that platform."

"Do you want some help from any of the butlers?" Thomas asked.

"No, I'll help," Clara declared. "This will be fun."

79

At quarter to seven, the Settlers' Club was ready for what could be its swan song. Dolly and Bah-Bah were on a gaily decorated platform in the club's window, the grand anniversary cake with all its tiers and ribbons and sprinkles rising proudly between them. The waiters were in the kitchen putting the final touches on trays of hors d'oeuvres. Maldwin was going over certain rules of etiquette with his students who were standing around in their formal dress, holding silver trays that would soon be filled with drinks. Classical music played on the stereo system, fake fires licked at fake logs in the fire-places, and Clara, wearing her short- sleeved floral dress and nice-but-sensible shoes, was on a ladder, fluffing the sheep's coats with a pick comb.

"Nat would be so proud of you," she said to them.

"Here, let me help."

Clara turned her head and looked down. It was Blaise, one of Maldwin's students. "Thank you, but no," she said firmly.

"Are you sure?" he asked.

"Don't I look sure? Besides, there's nothing left to do." She turned her back on him. It was dark outside, and she could see people stopping in front of the window to look at the sheep. Clara waved at them. "Hiiiii."

Down the block, Janey came scurrying with shopping bags full of desserts. She had already made one trip back to the club to assemble the pieces of the anniversary cake. By the time she got home and showered and changed, time had slipped away. Now she hurried into the Settlers' Club, up the steps and round the bend into the parlor.

"Clara!" she cried. "The sheep look great up there. I have two of their eyes that fell out! I forgot to put them back in."

Clara had just come down the ladder.

"Let me stick them back in!" Blaise offered.

"Why don't you help her with her bags?" Maldwin demanded.

Janey reached into her coat pocket and pulled out the two stones that had been retrieved from the floor of Jacques Harlow's loft. "I'd like to do it," she said as she handed the shopping bags to Blaise. "Here are the rest of the cakes and pies and cookies. Take them back to the kitchen, please."

Blaise trembled at the sight of the diamonds in Janey's hand. She darted over to the ladder and climbed up the steps. "Where's Thomas?" she asked Clara.

"Here I am, darling," Thomas announced from the doorway. "Let me help you with that."

"No, I'll do it myself. Dolly and Bah-Bah each lost an eye when they were away from home." Janey looked at the sheep. "But we found them, didn't we?" She reached over and stuck one of the stones in Dolly's left eye socket and the other in Bah-Bah's right eye socket. "Much better now!"

"Everything looks just perfect!" Clara declared. "Now we're ready to party."

80

Archibald was standing at the window across the street, binoculars in hand. "My God!" he cried. "The place is turning into a zoo!"

"What do you mean, dear?" Vernella said, emerging from the dressing room in a long gown and pearls.

Thorn came down the steps from his bedroom in a velvet smoking jacket. "What's this I hear?"

"They are pathetic! They have sheep in the window."

"Like a butcher shop!" Thorn said as he lit his pipe.

"I didn't think it could get much worse. But this time they've outdone themselves," Archibald said. "When I think of this park when I was a child. And to see it turn into a circus . . ."

Vernella put her arm around her husband's waist. "Don't worry, my dear. We'll change it back. When you buy the Settlers' Club, we'll be the King and Queen of Gramercy Park."

Archibald smiled slightly. "I suppose. And what will you be, Thorn?"

A little dribble formed in the corner of Thorn's mouth as he chewed on his pipe. I'll be the God of fire, he thought. "Oh, I suppose I'll just be a visiting prince."

Archibald laughed. "Not you, Thorn. You're much better suited to being a dictator. Now let's break out the champagne."

81

By seven-thirty the Settlers' Club was packed. Lydia's singles, club members, prospective club members, and Nora's group from the crime convention were all mingling and enjoying themselves. There were even adventurous types who had bought last-minute tickets to the party after reading about the festivities in the newspaper.

On the surface it looked like a successful party at a lovely club. But was it? Stanley was catching all the fun with his video camera, while the reporter who'd broken the scandalous story in the *New York World* hadn't dared to show up.

Regan was circulating, keeping an eye out for Georgette. So far there had been no sign of her. Clara was sipping a vodka martini. Thomas and Janey were doing their best to act as hosts. Lydia was chatting with a group in the corner, no doubt trying to recruit them for her own soirées. Maldwin watched over his butlers as they made sure everyone had a drink and was well taken care of. Daphne had not been seen at all. She had been so upset with Thomas about the sheep and her lost opportunity in Jacques Harlow's movies that Regan felt a little sorry for her.

Now if only Jack would get here, Regan thought as she joined the group around her mother and father.

"Those sheep are so interesting," Nora said. "I like them."

"So did the movie director who didn't want to give them back. I guess they're much more valuable than one might think at first glance."

"Their eyes do have a certain sparkle," Nora said.

Regan looked over and noticed a dark-haired woman hanging around by the sheep and occasionally staring up at them. Something about her seemed familiar, but Regan was sure she hadn't been at the singles party.

"Oh, here's Kyle Fleming," Nora said as she spotted Kyle coming through the door. "Regan, you should meet him. He gave the best lecture on con artists."

"I'd love to," Regan said.

* * *

Thomas was scheduled to give a toast right before they started the buffet line at eight. He went into his office to get out his notes. He'd worked hard on his little speech. If they were ever going to rustle up any new members for the club, now was the time to motivate them.

Thomas shut the door, walked over to his desk, and sat down. When he looked up, Daphne was leaning against the opposite wall, tears streaming down her cheeks.

"Daphne!"

"Can you come out back with me?" she asked, her voice cracking. "I need some air. I don't want anyone to see me like this."

"Of course!"

"Where's Thomas?" Janey asked Regan.

"I haven't seen him."

"He's not in his office and he's supposed to give a toast."

"Excuse me!"

Everyone turned to see a man who looked as if he'd had a few too many drinks climb the ladder near the sheep. He waved his arms at the crowd.

"I'd like to make an announcement," he slurred. "My name is Burkhard, and I know that some of you are here from Lydia Sevatura's sin-gles parties. I just thought that you should know that she has been making fun—"

"AAAAAHHHHHHHHH!" Lydia came charg-ing across the room like one of the bulls running in Pamplona and knocked down the ladder. Burkhard fell sideways, jostling the platform where the sheep were parked, and landed on top of the anniversary cake.

The sudden jolt dislodged one of Dolly's eyes, and it fell to the floor. As Regan rushed over, the dark-haired woman who'd been staring at the sheep dove for the ground, and an icing-covered Burkhard slid down on top of her.

Just as Regan leaned down to pull Burkhard up, she saw the woman's hand close over the eye. In a flash, everything came together. *I only have eyes for ewe.* The diamonds. The sparkly eyes.

"Buttercup!" Regan cried.

Georgette's head involuntarily turned toward Regan's voice.

"It's you, Georgette, isn't it?" Regan said. "Why don't you hand it over?"

With her free hand, Georgette reached down the inside of her leg, grabbed her gun, and start-ed to run for the door.

The crowd started to scream and scatter in a panic, trying to get out of Georgette's way.

With a burst of speed, Regan ran after her and tackled her from behind.

"No, Georgette," Regan yelled as the gun fired into the air, putting a hole through one of the ancient portraits above the stairway. Regan knocked the gun out of Georgette's hand as she wrestled her to the ground.

From behind Regan, the voice of Kyle Fleming boomed. "Georgette, how nice to see you again."

Georgette started screaming bloody murder as Regan grabbed the gun and pried the diamond from her hand. Kyle Fleming quickly slapped a pair of cuffs around Georgette's wrists.

With the diamond in hand, Regan raced back to the platform, raised the ladder off the floor, scrambled up the steps, and grabbed the three other diamonds from Dolly's and Bah-Bah's eye sockets. She turned to the crowd and held out her hand. "The missing diamonds!"

"The club is saved!" someone cried, and everyone cheered.

Just then, Janey's voice shouted from the doorway, "Regan, I can't find Thomas anywhere!"

Before Regan could say a word, Harriet came running out of the kitchen. *"Fire!"* she screamed and turned to run back.

Mass hysteria erupted once again. As it was, the crowd was packed in cheek by jowl. They turned as one and started heading for the door for the second time in a matter of moments.

Regan turned and saw Jack standing in the doorway. "Jack!"

"Regan, who was that woman who cried fire?"

"Harriet. One of the student butlers," Regan yelled, smoke pouring out all around.

Jack ran toward the kitchen.

"Regan, I have to find Thomas!" Janey wailed.

Nora and Luke were helping usher people out. Regan passed them. "Go ahead. We want to find Thomas. And I'm afraid there's someone else who might be in their apartment."

"I'm coming with you," Luke insisted.

Clara was nearby. "I'm coming too, Regan."

Together they all ran down the hall. Smoke was everywhere. "He's not in his office!" Regan yelled.

"Where is he?" Janey gasped.

Clara grabbed the master key from Thomas's desk.

"I'm going to try Daphne's door," Regan said. They raced down the hall, calling Thomas's and Daphne's names. Regan banged on the door to Daphne's apartment. "Give me the key," she ordered Clara.

Clara handed it over, and Regan unlocked the door. "Daphne," she called, turning on lights.

Peering into the bedroom, she saw clothes all over the bed. Is she under that rumpled mass? Regan wondered. She flicked on the light, raced over, Clara at her heels, and picked a sweater off the heap. No Daphne.

"Oh my God!" Regan yelled.

"Oh, sweet Jesus!" Clara cried.

There were two sheep appliqués stuck to the right arm of Daphne's sweater. "It was Daphne who killed Nat!" Regan said in horror.

Janey howled. "And she's furious with Thomas!"

"Let's go!" Regan said.

"I bet they're out back!" Clara cried.

They ran into the hallway, which was thick with smoke, and hurried down the staircase and out the back door. Daphne had Thomas cornered. She had a huge knife in her hands.

"Daphne!" Regan yelled.

Daphne turned to Regan, her eyes filled with hate. "He ruined my career!"

"What about Nat?" Regan asked, feeling for Georgette's gun in her jacket pocket.

"I was so good to him and Wendy. But after she died he only cared about his friends who played cards. I wanted him to be with me! But he said he could never be with another woman. Then he found somebody else. I know he did. And he had that big secret about the diamonds that he kept from me. I went crazy when I found out about that. He betrayed me!"

"Daphne, put down the knife," Regan pleaded.

"No!"

Thomas was quivering in the corner.

"Put it down."

After a moment, Daphne dropped the knife and started to cry, this time real tears. "I lost all my chances. Nat . . . my acting career . . ."

Thomas and Janey had yet another hug-filled reunion as Regan picked the knife off the ground. "Dad, could you hold this? I've got a phone call to make."

Regan pulled out her cell phone and called Edward Gold's home number. "Any chance you can get in here tonight with that certified check?" she asked him when he answered.

"What?" Thomas cried.

Regan held out her hand. The four diamonds were resting in her palm. Now it was Thomas's turn to cry. "They were in Dolly and Bah-Bah's eye sockets," Regan explained. "It's a good thing Janey brought them back."

Thomas turned to Janey. "Will you marry me?"

Back inside, the smoke was clearing. Regan hurried to find Jack. He was in the kitchen with Harriet, who was now in handcuffs.

"Regan," Jack said softly and put his arms around her.

Finally it's my turn, Regan thought.

"Our butler here was doing her best to spread the fire," Jack informed her. "Now I've got to visit her boyfriend, Thorn, who is staying across the street. They've been working as a team to destroy any butler schools that compete with them. Because they thought no one would recognize her here in New York, she posed as a butler student."

Harriet scowled at him.

Maldwin was in the corner of the kitchen, trying to help clean up the mess. "I should have known that Thorn would try to infiltrate my school. He never liked me," he said. "But I'll show him. I'm going to keep going with my school. At least three of my butlers were good people," he said.

"Make that two," Kyle Fleming called from the doorway. "I'd been looking for that Blaise character for a while. We got him detained out front too."

Maldwin almost collapsed.

Across the way, Vernella and Archibald were astounded by the smoke.

"The place is on fire!" Vernella cried.

"That's awful!" Archibald said. "I want them

to close, but I don't want people to get hurt. Not to mention the smoke damage to my building!"

In the commotion outside, they saw someone hurrying across the street. Their doorbell rang. Vernella and Archibald looked at each other.

It was Jack Reilly.

"Can I help you?" Archibald asked him.

"Is Thorn Darlington here?"

"Cousin Thorn is upstairs."

"I'm here to place him under arrest for conspiring to commit arson."

Archibald whirled around. Thorn was standing at the top of the stairs. "You've ruined our family's good name!" he cried. "Ruined it!"

"And our chance to be the King and Queen of Gramercy Park," Vernella snarled as she rushed to grab the champagne flute from Thorn's hand.

An hour later, the party was back on inside the club. It was safe to say that the smoke had cleared. Edward Gold arrived with his wife, carrying a huge certified check for four million dollars made out to the Settlers' Club. "We would have gotten here sooner, but there was a lot of traffic."

"Sooner!" his wife exclaimed. "He drove like a madman!"

As the crowd gathered around, Thomas

climbed the ladder in front of the sheep to make the toast.

Everyone raised their glass. Regan and Jack stood arm in arm by the fireplace with Clara next to them. Nora and Luke were there with the crime-convention people. Lydia was with her singles, her arms draped around two of them like a mother bear with her cubs. Burkhard had been banished from the premises, cake crumbs and icing stuck to his one good suit. Maldwin stood between his loyal butlers, Vinnie and Albert, who suddenly looked more butlerish. Janey stood adoringly at Thomas's feet, and the club members filled out the crowd, suddenly prouder than ever to be part of such an establishment.

Stanley was ecstatic as his camera rolled. My special's going to be unbelievable, he thought.

"I'd like to toast the memory of Nat and Ben. Thanks to them the Settlers' Club will live on. We will all continue to be together for many years to come as we live, work, and thrive inside these smoky walls."

Everyone laughed and took a sip of their vintage champagne as Dolly and Bah-Bah stood guard over the club.

Nora and Luke and Kyle were standing together.

"We're going to have a lot to talk about at the brunch tomorrow," Nora said.

"Too bad we can't have our friend Georgette appear in person." Kyle laughed.

"In one of her disguises," Luke added.

Jack turned to Regan and smiled. "Now, where were we?"

Regan smiled back. "I think we were planning a trip to California."

"I can't wait," he said.

"Me neither." Their hands became entwined.

"Ya know," Clara announced as she practically planted herself between them, "my sister and I went out to California just last year. Oh, it was lovely . . ."

Jack squeezed Regan's hand.

I really can't wait, Regan thought, as she smiled and squeezed his hand back.

"Now have you ever driven down the Coast?" Clara continued. "Gorgeous. Just gorgeous. You two should try it . . ."

Pocket Star Books
proudly presents

BURNED

Carol Higgins Clark

Coming in June 2006 in paperback
from Pocket Star Books

Turn the page for a preview of *Burned* . . .

1

Thursday, January 13

"This is going to be the snowstorm of the century," the action reporter, Brad Dayton, cried with a certain hysterical glee. Clad in bright yellow foul weather gear, he was standing on the side of the New Jersey Turnpike. Cars were inching by, sliding and spinning, as a gusty wind blew wet snow in every direction. The flakes seemed to target the reporter's face and the lens of the television camera. The sky was thick with gray clouds, and the whole Northeast was hunkering down for an unexpected blizzard.

"Don't go anywhere," he cried as he blinked to avoid the pelting precipitation. "Stay home. And forget the airports. They're closed, and it looks like they won't reopen for several days."

Regan Reilly stared at the television in her cozy Los Angeles office in an ancient building on Hollywood Boulevard. "I can't believe it," she said aloud. "I should have flown out yesterday."

"Be careful out there, Brad," urged the cable news anchor in the climate-controlled studio. "Try to stay dry."

"I will," Brad shouted over the shrill wind. He started to say something else, but the sound was knocked out. The news director cut quickly to a weatherman standing in front of a map with lots of ominous arrows pointing in all directions.

"What have you got for us, Larry?" the smiling blond anchorwoman asked.

"Snow coming from all directions," Larry explained urgently as his hands made circles around the map. "Snow, snow, and more snow. I hope you all have lots of canned goods at home because this storm is going to stay with us for the next several days, and it is packing a *wallop!*"

Regan looked out the window. It was a typically sunny day in Los Angeles. Her suitcase was packed for New York. Recently engaged, Regan was a thirty-one-year-old private investigator based in Los Angeles. Her honey, Jack "no relation" Reilly, was the head of the major case squad in New York City. They were to wed in May, and she had been planning to fly out for the weekend to see Jack and her parents, Luke and Nora, who lived in Summit, New Jersey.

Regan and her mother were supposed to meet with a wedding coordinator on Saturday to review all the plans for the big day—menu, flowers, limos, photographer, the list went on and on. On Saturday night she and her parents and Jack had arranged to hear a band they were considering for the reception. Regan had been looking forward to a fun night out. The snowstorm would have precluded those plans, but if Regan had gotten to New York yesterday, she could have had a cozy weekend with Jack. It was the second week in January, and she hadn't seen him for ten days. And what's more romantic than being together during a snowstorm?

She felt lonely and frustrated, and the sight of the shining sun she found irritating. I don't want to be here, she thought. I want to be in New York.

The phone rang.

"Regan Reilly," she answered without much enthusiasm.

"Aloha, Regan. It's your maid of honor calling from Hawaii."

Kit Callan was Regan's best friend. They'd met in college on a junior year abroad program in England. Kit lived in Hartford and sold insurance. Her other job was the hunt for Mr. Right. So far she was having better luck peddling her policies.

"Aloha, Kit." Regan smiled and immediately felt better just hearing her best friend's voice. She knew that Kit had gone to Hawaii for an insurance convention. "How's your trip going?"

"I'm stuck here."

"Not many people would complain that they were stuck in Hawaii."

"The convention ended Tuesday. I took an extra day to relax, and now I can't get home. My travel agent says you can't get anywhere near the East Coast."

"Tell me about it. I was supposed to go to New York today to see Jack. And my mother and I were going to meet with the wedding planner."

"Promise me you'll go easy on me with the bridesmaids' dresses."

"I was actually thinking of plaid pantsuits," Regan quipped.

"I've got an idea. Come out here, and we'll pick up some grass skirts."

Regan laughed. "Now there's an idea. People always want their weddings to be different."

"So you're coming then?"

"What are you talking about?"

"Get out here, Regan! How many chances will we have to be together like this again? Once you get hitched, that'll be it. You'll never want to leave him, and I don't blame you."

"I'm keeping my office in Los Angeles," Regan protested. "At least for a while."

"That's different. You know what I mean. This is a perfect opportunity for us to have a fun girls' weekend before your wedding. What else are you going to do for the next few days? Watch the weather reports? Come out here to Waikiki. I'll have a tropical drink waiting for you. I have a room on the second floor with two big beds and a balcony overlooking the ocean. You can almost dip your toes into the sand from here. As a matter of fact, I'm sitting on the balcony right now waiting for room service to deliver my breakfast."

"Be careful. With the sound of the waves crashing, you might not hear them knock," Regan muttered as she looked around the office that had been her home away from home for several years. The antique desk she'd found at a flea market, the black-and-white-tiled floor, the coffeepot in its place of honor atop a filing cabinet were all so familiar. But now they didn't feel welcoming. She had cleared the decks for a weekend away and felt the need to get out and go somewhere. It was true that she hadn't seen Kit much in the year since she'd met Jack.

"Where are you staying?" Regan asked.

"The Waikiki Waters Playground and Resort."

"That's a mouthful."

"You should see this place. It was just renovated, so everything is brand-new and beautiful. There are restaurants, shops, two spas, five pools, and several towers of rooms. We're in the best tower right on the water. And there's a gala charity ball this Saturday night. They're auctioning off a shell lei that belonged to a princess from the royal family. They're calling it the 'Be a Princess' Ball. So come on out. We'll both be princesses." Kit paused. "What's going on down there?" she said softly, more to herself than Regan.

"What are you talking about?" Regan asked.

Kit didn't seem to hear her. "I don't believe it," she said with alarm.

Regan's grip tightened on the phone. "Kit, what's going on?"

"People are suddenly running down to the water's edge. I think a body just washed ashore!"

"Are you kidding?"

"A woman just tore out of the water screaming her head off. It looks like she came across the body when she was out for a swim."

"Oh, my God."

"Regan, you're not going to let me stay by myself here this weekend, are you?" Kit inquired meekly. "This place could be dangerous."

"I'll call the airlines."

2

Nora Regan Reilly looked up at the snow falling on the skylight of her third-floor tower office at home in New Jersey. Normally a little snow would contribute to the cozy setting where she wrote her mystery novels. But the blizzard was causing havoc in her life and, it seemed, everyone else's in the tri-state area.

"Regan, I'm so sorry you won't be in New York this weekend."

"Me, too, Mom." Regan was in the bedroom of her Hollywood Hills apartment packing a suitcase with summer clothes.

"Hawaii doesn't sound so bad."

"It will be good to spend time with Kit. Things

have been so busy, I know I'd never take a weekend like this otherwise."

"Your father has a big funeral scheduled for tomorrow. I don't know how it can possibly happen. They say the roads will be treacherous. Most of the relatives are from out of town. They're staying at a hotel nearby."

"Who died?" Regan's question was not an uncommon one at the Reillys' dinner table. Her father, Luke, was a funeral director. And with her mother, Nora, being a suspense writer, there was a lot of talk about crime and death around the house. The Waltons they were not. Regan was an only child, and as a result she had been privy to more adult conversations than most kids growing up. It seemed to be common with only children, Regan had long ago decided. Jack was one of six kids. She loved that. Soon they'd have the best of both worlds.

"Ernest Nelson. He just turned a hundred and had been a championship skier. He lived in an assisted-living facility in town, and his family is scattered all over. His wife just died last year."

"He was one hundred years old?"

"He celebrated his hundredth birthday in a very grand style two weeks ago. The family threw him a big party. Now they're all back to bury him. And there are a lot of them. He has eight children who all have numerous grandchildren. I think they're going to be here for a while."

"He sounds like the type who wanted to reach that milestone before he gave up. Somehow the weather seems fitting for his funeral."

"That's what they're all saying, Regan." Nora paused. "Have you told Jack your plans?"

"Of course. We're both disappointed that I'm not in New York for the storm, but I'll be there next weekend."

"How long will you stay in Hawaii?" Nora asked as she sipped steaming tea from the *Imus in the Morning* mug she was given the last time she was on his radio show.

"Just until Monday morning."

"Do you and Kit have any big plans out there?"

Regan dropped a red one-piece bathing suit into her suitcase. With her pale skin she wasn't a sun worshipper, but she did enjoy taking a dip and then sitting under an umbrella. She had inherited her black Irish looks from her father. Raven-haired, blue-eyed, and fair-skinned, she was five feet seven inches tall. Luke was six-foot-five and his hair was "long since silver," as he liked to call it. Her mother was a petite blond and had a more patrician look. "We'll sit on the beach, maybe do some sightseeing. I think Kit has her eye on a guy who lives in Waikiki."

"She does?"

"Well, she mentioned something about a few people she met who have retired young out there or gone to start second careers. One of them sounds interesting."

"Kit's probably happy she can't get home then."

"I think you're right, Mom. She only admitted it to me when I called her back with my flight information. But as she said, a long-distance relationship takes on new meaning when you're talking about Connecticut to Hawaii."

Nora laughed. "I'm sure you two will have fun. Be careful in the water. Those currents out there can get pretty strong."

She has that Irish intuition, Regan marveled. Or was it her motherly radar? Regan was not going to mention that a body had washed ashore in front of Kit's hotel room, but her mother probably had a sense of something. When Regan had called Kit back, Kit was down on the beach. The body had been identified as Dorinda Dawes, a woman in her forties who was an employee of the Waikiki Waters. She had started there three months ago and was the hotel's roving photographer and reporter, in charge of their newsletter. Kit had met her at one of the bars at the hotel where Dorinda was taking pictures of the guests.

When she washed ashore, Dorinda wasn't wearing a bathing suit. She was wearing a tropical print dress and had a shell lei around her neck. Which meant she wasn't out for a casual swim.

No, Regan had decided. No sense mentioning it to her mother. Let Nora think she was going to have a relaxing weekend at a peaceful Hawaiian resort. Who knows? Maybe things would turn out that way after all.

But knowing her pal Kit, she somehow doubted it. Kit could find trouble at a church picnic. And once again it looked as if she had. Sometimes Regan thought that's why they were such good friends. In their own ways, they both had an affinity for the hazardous side of life.

"We'll be careful," Regan assured her mother.

"Stick together. Especially when you're swimming."

"We will." Regan hung up, zipped up her suitcase, and glanced at the picture of her and Jack on the dresser. It had been taken moments after they got engaged in a hot air balloon. Regan couldn't believe how lucky she was to have found her soul mate. They'd met when her father had been kidnapped and Jack was on the case. Now Luke always joked that he never knew he had such good matchmaking skills—after all, Regan and Jack got to know each other while he was tied up on a boat with his chauffeur. But they were terrific together and had so much in common, especially their senses of humor. What they both did for a living also made them kindred spirits, and they often discussed their cases with each other. She had dubbed him "Mr. Feedback." At the end of every conversation he always told her he loved her and to *be careful!*

"I will, Jack," she said now to the picture. "I want to live to wear my wedding dress." But somehow as Regan spoke the words aloud, they seemed to get caught in her throat. Brushing off the odd feeling of uneasiness that came over her, Regan pulled the suitcase off the bed and headed out the door. Here I go on my bachelorette weekend, she thought. How bad can it be?

3

As Regan's plane made its descent into Honolulu, she peered out the window and smiled at the sight of the red neon letters on top of the airport tower—A-L-O-H-A.

"Aloha," she murmured.

When she got off the plane, a rush of warm fragrant air hit her. She immediately pulled out her cell phone and called Jack. It was late in the evening in New York.

"Aloha, baby," Jack answered.

Regan smiled again. "Aloha. I just arrived. The sky is bright blue. I can spot a row of palm trees swaying in the breeze, a pagoda in a garden below, and I really wish you were with me."

"Me, too."

"What's happening in New York?"

"The snow is coming down fast and furious. I had a couple of drinks with the guys after work. People are out on the streets having a great time, throwing snowballs and pulling kids on sleds. Someone already built a snowman that is standing guard outside my building. But he doesn't have much to do. Crime goes down during snowstorms."

Regan felt a pang in her heart. "I can't believe I'm missing all that," she said wistfully.

"I can't believe you are, either."

Regan pictured Jack's spacious homey apartment that was so Jack with its handsome leather couches and beautiful Persian rugs. He had told Regan he wanted to make his place more than just a bachelor pad because he never knew when he'd meet the right girl. "I was afraid it might never happen," he admitted. "But with you this is finally the way it's supposed to be."

"Maybe there will be another snowstorm next weekend," Regan joked. "I'll just be sure to arrive ahead of it."

"Regan, have a good time with Kit. There will be other snowstorms, I promise. And believe me, a lot of people in this city would give anything to trade places with you right now. Not everyone thinks this is fun."

By now Regan was at the baggage claim. People

were in shorts and sleeveless shirts. It was late afternoon, and there was a laid-back, peaceful feeling in the air.

"I'll be fine," Regan said. "Kit met some people out here who we'll hook up with. There's even a guy she likes."

"Uh-oh."

"Uh-oh is right. But this one sounds promising. He worked on Wall Street and retired to Hawaii at age thirty-five."

"Maybe I should run a check on him," Jack suggested. He laughed, but there was a note of seriousness in his voice. "He sounds too good to be true." Jack was fond of Kit and felt protective of her. A couple of the guys Kit had gotten involved with since Jack had been on the scene had been real lulus. He wanted to make sure whoever she dated was on the level.

"It won't be long before I learn his name and hear every detail of his life that Kit knows already. I'll fill you in. If you find something out about him that's not so great, she'll want to be told. She learned her lesson from that last loser she went out with."

"She sure did," Jack agreed.

They were referring to a guy Kit had several dates with who failed to mention that he was getting married and moving to Hong Kong.

"Hey, Regan," Jack continued. "I have a buddy out there in the Honolulu police force. I'll give him a call and let him know you're there. Maybe he'll have some suggestions about what to do or where to go."

"That's great. What's his name?" Regan asked as she pulled her suitcase off the carousel. She was always amazed at how connected Jack was. He knew people everywhere. And everyone respected him.

"Mike Darnell. I got to know him when some of the guys and I used to go there on vacation."

"I'm about to grab a cab to the hotel," Regan said as she wheeled her luggage outside.

"Don't have too good of a time."

"How could I? You're not here."

"I love you, Regan."

"I love you, too, Jack."

"Be careful, Regan."

"I will."

The cabdriver tossed Regan's suitcase into the trunk. Regan got in the back, and they sped off for the Waikiki Waters. So much for being careful, Regan thought as the taxi driver dodged in and out of traffic on the congested highway. Regan found it odd that the road was called Interstate H1. Where were the other states?

Six thousand miles away Jack hung up and

looked around his apartment. "This place is so lonesome without her," he said aloud. But he cheered himself with the thought that she'd be there with him in one week. So what was that nagging feeling that came over him? He tried to shrug it off. He was a worrier when it came to Regan. And now he had a particularly good reason. Whenever she was with Kit, something odd always happened.

Jack stood and walked over to the window. The snow was piling up quickly. He walked across the room to his desk, got out his address book, and dialed his friend in the Honolulu Police Department. But the conversation only made him feel worse. Regan hadn't told him anything about the drowning of a hotel employee at the Waikiki Waters. There was no way Kit wouldn't have mentioned it to her. Regan knows me too well, he thought.

"Mike, would you do me a favor and give Regan a call?"

"Of course, Jack. I've got to run into a meeting. I'll talk to you later."

Standing by his window, Jack watched the snow coming down on the darkened street. I'll feel so much better when she's *Mrs.* Reilly, he thought. He turned, went into his room, and lay on the bed.

Back in Waikiki, people couldn't stop talking about the death of Dorinda Dawes.